IT'S MERE FOLLY

1.

The year for the boys started on the first Friday of the new year. At first it was the novelty of a drink on their way home from work; now twenty-three years later, many changes of venue and into their retirement, the weekly meeting continued in fact it developed into a habit.

The four of them had all worked in the metropolis thirty minutes to the south of the bedroom community of Mere Folly a small city of some fifty thousand people.

Anything and everything that they had or achieved, had been worked for and therefore, at their stage in life they weren't too concerned in saying what they thought.

They had been through the good times and bad. They had had good experiences and bad. They had experienced good people and bad. The honeya quote, "Some people will only "love you" as much as they can use you. Their loyalty ends where the benefits stop" basically summed up many people that they had met and worked with during their business lives.

In essence, they only echoed what many people thought; whether it be local, regional or national politics, about taxpayer subsidized radio and tv operations having political affiliations or the bozo living in his free mansion who has never lived in the real world.

The slower pace of retirement life gave them time to stew over the inane bureaucrats and politicians around them.

The servers in the various hostelries they had habituated over the years had come to call them the "boys" even to the extent of giving them the odd free drink "odd" meaning rare or infrequent not peculiar. The four of them had been using this latest venue, not far from where they lived, for a couple of years. With their humour, sarcasm and wit, they became a bit of an institution at Florence, better known as Flo's.

Good times never seem to last for ever, that's why every couple of years, the boys changed venue, Flo's was no exception. Just when they had developed a comfort zone, a new manager arrived and almost immediately things started to go sour. It started when he deemed himself too busy to meet them as he was too busy chatting up a waitress.

'You know, he's a right bloody wally' remarked the Bert, making sure that he could hear him.

The boys were all retired, they had been around, had lots of business experience and street smarts. All they wanted was a local watering hole where they felt comfortable and could relax. Then as they discussed, an arrogant little toad comes on board and single-handed starts to dismantle any atmosphere and comfort that existed.

The wally had been managing one of Mario's hospitality places in downtown Mere Folly.

The building had been around for years in various guises; the latest being a knock off of an Irish pub. Renovations were just completed, in fact the boys were invited to the opening.

It wasn't that Mario didn't trust anybody but he really didn't trust anybody, especially his staff and especially his staff in a new venture's very early days. Mario was in the pub literally all the time and was there when Tom, Bert, Kev and Jim walked in. The boys had known Mario off and on, more off than on, for many years so they thought that they would give his latest venture a try. Mario was his usual excitable self and thrilled to see his old buddies again.

'Come and see this.'
'What do you think?'
'Think about what.'
'The new room. The George Best room.'
'The who room?'

George Best, the greatest Irish football player ever.'

There it was, Mario had renovated a room in the pub and placed a sign above the door.

The George Best Room; it was decked out with pictures and all sorts of memorabilia.

'What do you think?'

There was silence.

'Mario, George Best is Scottish'.

There was stunned silence. Mario went pale'

'No, you clown, he's Irish.'

'Mario, who told you, that, an Irishman?'

'I've got to go but I will sort it out, somebody's going to pay for this.'

For the next couple of hours, the boys couldn't stop laughing. Normally they would only see Mario once every couple months, but they knew he would definitely be there the following Friday.

'Perhaps we should go somewhere else then.'

'No way, I want to see his face, I'm really looking forward to seeing it when he finds out Besty actually is Irish'

Sure enough, Mario was there waiting for them.

'You bastards,' he is Irish.

'Indeed, he is'

'You idiots told me he was Scotch,'

'No Mario, scotch is a drink, people from Scotland are Scottish, but Besty is Irish.

'I told you that,' laughed Mario.

They christened the George Best room with Irish Beer, an Italian, a Canadian and three Englishmen.

The boys were still invited to the official opening on one condition. If they opened their mouths about the George Best Room, they would be turfed out the door and banned. For the sake of free beer and food, silence was golden.

The place never lived up to expectations, the staff were devoid of personality, there was no atmosphere, Mario's visits declined, he was a busy guy, other projects took his interest and time. Eventually he was never there so the boys moved on Anyway, time went by, managers came and went at the pub, the place was never very full, the takings were driven down especially with the wally managing the place

Mario couldn't believe his luck when one day he got an offer for the pub. A couple of Irishmen bought it. They needed a hobby, something to get them out of the house and the ability to write off the cost of their beer. It didn't take them long to figure out that the manager was a real dipstick and punted him.

Coincidentally, the manager at Flo's literally disappeared. Mario, urgently needing a manager and feeling sorry for the wally, gave him the job.

As he did in his previous role, the wally wandered around aimlessly, doing nothing except trying to chat up the waitresses. The waitresses did not stay long, they weren't happy being propositioned. In addition, they were not happy having a middle-aged lecher as a boss, looking at them through his bottle bottomed glasses trying to intimidate and bully them if they didn't show an interest in him

Most nights of the week the bar at Flo's was relatively empty but it was always very busy on a Friday night with people sat in the foyer waiting for a table in the small intimate bar.

The boys had been moaning for years that as regulars they should get a reserved table, but no dice. As usual with these places regulars are never looked after when times are good, the boys were getting a bit disgruntled and a change of venue was brought up. Old habits die hard as the servers were good and did have personalities and other attributes, unlike the new manager.

A new place down the road had been a topic of conversation for a couple of weeks. All they needed was a nudge to try it, this was it. The following week they were down the road at Chat another new venture put together by Mario. The new venue was a European style café with cheap chairs and tables. It was a bit more up market than the hamburger and coffee joints that discouraged comfort in order to get the clientele in and out. The café was a bit more comfortable; not that much, as again it didn't want to encourage people to stay all night, unless that is they kept eating and drinking. However, most people had their meal and a drink and then sat around for ages with a cup of coffee while fresh customers were being turned away. Restaurateurs all think that their clients know nothing about food, they probably don't, that's what keeps certain restaurants in business. Chat was no different. It was its newness and location that attracted people. Certainly not the food. As the boys would say, "you can't really mess up a pizza as long as you don't burn it".

After a couple of months and relatively full tables, the old restaurant trick of gradually sliding the prices up was applied. This didn't go un noticed by the boys and talk of another venue started. Kev was the major stirrer, always there to give advice, interrupting whoever was trying to make a point, never wrong, in fact bullshit baffled brains. He was always telling the boys that he had spilt wine down his pants in more places across the world than they could ever have dreamed of. Jim made a habit of sticking his finger down his throat so often at Kev's tales that Tom and Bert took it for granted.

Then, surprise, surprise; Charley, who used to manage Flo's up the road before the wally, was stood behind the bar, he saw the boys arrive and wandered over.

'We wondered what happened to you. What are you doing here?'

'I had an offer I couldn't refuse and now own 50% of this place'

At last, a place which had a manager with personality, they all hugged and shook Charley's hand

'So that means, as the owner you can keep this table for us from 3 till 6 every Friday.'

'Gentlemen, no problem.'

To cement the relationship glasses of Sambuca appeared on the table, which further endeared the boys to him, but not that much. The increase in prices was raised. Charley was apologetic and even more so when he was reminded that supposedly drinks and food should be cheaper, not more expensive during happy hour.

'How come beer had gone up by some fifty percent.'

'Not my decision'

'It had to be fifty percent your decision,' said Tom.

I do have control over these though as amuse-gueule arrived. Charley explained that they were not on the menu, chosen specifically, created by the chef and offered gratis.

'Condescending prick' smiled Bert, 'but we will take all he throws at us'

As they sat there, drinking their third free Sambuca, the increase in beer prices didn't seem to matter. That would be until the bill for the beer arrived.

One thing did hit them as they chatted away. They were rather bemused and felt it rather odd that Mario would give away 50% of one of his places. Admittedly, Charley was family, but also knowing Mario giving away 50% just didn't make sense.

Time passed, even though they brought up the extortionate beer prices every week they had a comfort zone and got used to Sambuca on the house every Friday

One Tuesday evening Bert popped his head in to pick up some lasagna. 'This is a restaurant, isn't it?' inquired Bert,
The waiter looked puzzled, 'So why haven't you got lasagna'

'Unfortunately, we ordered it from our central kitchen and it hasn't turned up yet,'

Bert was still on a mission, 'are you sure this is a cafe, do you sell hamburgers?' The waiter relaxed and smiled, 'We can do that for you sir'

'I can go over the road if I want a hamburger. If I want lasagna I go to a cafe where it is on the menu. This is a cafe with lasagna on the menu, isn't it? so if you have bloody hamburgers why haven't you got lasagna and walked out'

The following Friday, as soon as Charley sat down with the boys. Bert was on it again "have you got any lasagna yet"

"Let me" but he was cut short by Bert, "Oh I don't want any I just want to know if this cafe has lasagna"

Well Charley wasn't happy, he got up and left, there was no Sambuca that night

The next week Bert was back on his tirade. As Charley breezed by Bert made sure he heard his comment about lasagna which wasn't too complimentary, guess what no Sambuca

Bert was bent out of shape, 'if he can't take a joke that's hi problem, we'll go elsewhere.'

'Where?'

'Well that new place over the road'

The following week Bert couldn't make it, but he still expected the others to go over the road, however the remaining three decided to meet as usual to see if the atmosphere remained toxic, if it did, they would walk over the road.

Charley kept looking over and when he was certain Bert wasn't coming in he wandered over with glasses of Sambuca and sat with them.

My apologies guys for last week but if Bert had of made one more comment about lasagna I wouldn't have been responsible for my actions

'No problem, we totally get it, we were getting embarrassed too'

The week after, Bert was making comments on how they were chickening out of going over the road
'Listen you dufus you were like a gramophone record. We got Sambucas and an apology last week.'
'Only because I wasn't there'
'Exactly, so if you mention bloody lasagna again….'
Bless his cotton socks Charley came across, Bert apologized they kissed and made up, Sambucas followed

There was the odd occasion when somebody couldn't make it, but every Friday at around 3.30 p.m. they arrived to take advantage of happy hour. They donated their weekly $10 to the lottery fund with winnings over the years accumulating to $305 and donations to the lottery fund mega thousands.
After a couple of beers, as usual, they were dreaming of what they would do with a few million dollars.
'Its only $12 million this week' said Bert 'not worth winning'
'That's ok, the rest of us will take the $4 million each, you have too much money anyway'.
That's how it was, the repartee never stopped.
So, the Boys carried on reminiscing, taking the piss and telling stories as their fresh beers arrived…

2.

The boys were neighbors, they were sat on Bert's deck and just happened to be discussing Percy's crows. Percy, who had been seventy from birth lived next door to Bert. Bert, in turn lived next door to Tom, whilst Jim and Kev lived across the road. Tom had wandered round to Bert's for a beer, Kev and Jim were already there.

'Tell them about your gun,' "piss off" said Bert, he knew he should have only got it out when his neighbours weren't around to tease him.

Bert was self-conscious as he told them about the little pellet gun he had picked up at the store. He knew that he was going to be ridiculed.

This isn't Texas, we don't shoot burglars around here.

'I'm fed up with Percy's bloody crows so I got this gun and shot at one of them. I put some apple on the deck, sure enough it took it and took it on to the roof over there and missed him. I thought that crows were smart, but no it came back for another piece flew up there again and this time I nailed him.'

There it was a big black crow lying motionless on the roof, it wasn't exactly sun bathing.

Bert went to get a ladder, when he came back they sat chuckling as he put it up against the house climbed up and grabbed the dead crow. 'I can't leave it there, can I?'

The boys were all cracking up listening to the story. They thought that he was going to put it into the garbage, but Bert had a better idea. He went up Percy's drive and stuck the dead bird in Percy's mailbox with its head sticking out

'Sooner or later, he will get the message, if he wants to feed vermin peanuts then he should keep them in his own yard'

Then Bert nipped into his house and came back with a piece of paper and envelope. Computer generated print read "anytime they leave your yard they will be returned by mail, have a good day. Percy may like the vermin squawking at 4 in the morning, frightening off the small birds, raiding their nests, banging on roofs etc. etc.'

He then wedged the envelope into the crow's mouth and tied the it closed with a piece of string.

The boys regarded Percy as a prick and had had enough of him and his eccentricities, but they were confident that there were always two ways to skin a crow.

Next day Tom walked past Percy's house, the mail had been received as the mail box lid was down. He sat on Bert's deck looking into Percy's garden. There was the idiot emptying more peanuts into various containers, Bert could not understand it as the only things that he attracted to his garden were crows and squirrels and they could look after themselves

Percy always went out Monday, Wednesday and Friday. Wednesday morning just before he left he put out chunks of apple and peanuts, as soon as he was gone the crows flew from the giant fir tree and took them to the "safety" of the roof

When Percy got home there was more 'mail' in his mailbox waiting for him. Bert and Tom were at the front of Bert's house when Percy walked by to get his regular mail from the super mailboxes down the street.

'Someone has been playing nasty tricks' he said

'What do you mean?' they asked very innocently?

Percy, quite harmlessly told them that crows had been left in his mailbox

They chuckled, as they told Kev and Jim

You should have said, 'Would you believe it!!, it looks like Canada Post is delivering to our doors again.'

'Well, a bird in the house mailbox is worth two in the super mailbox'.

'That's nothing to crow about' added Jim

They were all breaking up laughing with tears welling in their eyes.

It didn't stop when Bert brought out another round.

'Stop squawking and get that down you'

Next day, Tom and Bert were outside as Percy went to get his mail.

'Morning Percy, any more packages' yelled Bert

He told them that they were very funny as he got his mail and walked back to his house oblivious as to who or why there were crows being stuffed in his mailbox. They couldn't take it any longer, so they shouted back at Percy.

'Why do you think that those crows are stuffed in your mailbox. '

'Probably some kids having a good time' said Percy.

'No, your dipstick, people round here are fed up with those vermin squawking at 4 in the morning and frightening other birds off.'

'Well, that's nature' said Percy as he joined them. 'I can't help that.

'Of course you can, you are feeding them and encouraging them to stay, that's not nature.'

'Oh, I never thought of it in that way,'

'Of course you didn't'

'What do you think I should do.'

'Stop bloody feeding them.'

'But they live in my tree,' said Percy.

'They wouldn't if you didn't feed them'
'They are vermin Percy, the city doesn't like them either, they will come and get rid of them for you,'

'Are you sure?' said Percy.

'Of course, we are sure'.
'I didn't realize that I was upsetting my neighbors' said Percy, 'why didn't you say something'

'We have for years, but you just ignored us and kept giving them peanuts.'

Three days later a City of Mere Folly van was on Percy's drive.

At Chat that evening, the boys decided that they should have Percy over for a beer,'

Bert was amazed. 'Why he said. In the thirty years of living there Percy has never made the effort to be neighborly despite his position as president of the neighborhood watch.'

'It takes two to tango,' said Kev. 'At our time of life, fault shouldn't be a concern, let's get together with him sooner rather than later, maybe he's a nice guy deep down.'

'He probably is, look at the work he does for the community. I mean he's always working with the police'

After two beers Percy started to open up. They were discovering that deep down Percy was a lonely man. He was involved in various organizations, strictly to keep busy and meet people, but there was never any lasting relationship.

There was a hint of empathy. Out of curiosity, or perhaps snooping, they were trying to see what his plans were going forward

"I would really like to sell this place. I have been taking a look at the senior's residence over on the highway."

'Is that what you really want?'

'I've had enough of it round here' said Percy as he started on his third beer, 'nobody round here appreciates what I do or ask my advice. Nobody round here knows what they want. The police are always telling me that I should be helping them more.'

'You do a fair bit round here, they should be paying you. '

'Well, they do' said Percy.

'How come', gulped Kev a little surprised.

'Well,' said Percy, feeling good to be one of the boys. The alcohol helped as well. 'Anything that I hear or see, I drop them an e mail and keep them updated.'

'So, you're their eyes and ears on any vandalism and that kind of stuff,' asked Jim. 'Well sort of, but what they really need is any kind of gossip,'

'What do you mean, gossip', asked Jim.

'It's amazing what you pick up at some of those meetings' said Percy.

'But Percy, you are on neighborhood and community committees not the board of the mafia. What kind of information can you give to the police from those meetings that can't be read in the minutes?' asked Kev.

'That's where you are wrong,' he said, getting agitated, but managing to take another beer from Tom.

'That's where you're bloody wrong Mr. know it all'.

All of a sudden, the boys were seeing a new autocratic Percy. 'The police rely on people like me. Only last week I was telling them of a guy on the community committee who was cheating on his wife.'

What's that got to do with bloody police' shouted Kev angrily.

'Aaah Mr. bloody know it all' said Percy, getting less and less coherent, 'the police really thanked me.'

'Why would they do that, aren't you wasting their time' said Bert, 'they actually pay you for telling them things like that.'

'Of course,' said Percy, 'they told me that they would have words with them.'

'Why' said Bert 'they're not exactly bloody marriage counselors.'

'Who was this guy? asked Tom.

'Looking around to make sure nobody was eavesdropping,' Percy whispered, 'would you believe our city manager. I could hear him chatting away with this lady. Disgusting' he said.

'Percy this stuff goes on all the time' said Kev, 'it doesn't make him a criminal, why report it to the cops?'

'Obvious isn't it', shouted back Percy, 'Disgusting, its adultery'.

'How do you know; suppose you were taking it out of context?'

'He was saying that his wife was away, how would she like to come out to dinner."

'Percy you are a right prick, I've done that with my wife's friend, that doesn't mean I was going to bed with her afterwards'

'Do you tell the police about all the gossip you hear? look at the monthly meetings you go to at the cop shop. I appreciate what you are doing, but come on Percy, Gord down the street told us about that evening he went with you, he said it was a joke. You were trying to get them to publish the crime statistics but they kept on ignoring you and actually he was embarrassed. As the cops are a canned culture, it was their way or no way. They just are not prepared to listen to outsiders, let's face it the only reason they have these meetings and pop in to things like the neighborhood watch parties is optics and perception. They are using you!'

'I knew it, I knew it said Percy you are all the bloody same, he put his bottle down and staggered down the deck stairs'

'What do you make of that,' said Kev. There's a guy who gives his heart and soul to the community, and he is being used by the cops, but he's too damn simple and stupid to realize that.'

'Well he is a banker.'

'Ah now I understand and obviously, that's why the cops are using him said Tom

3.

Earlier, the mayor and his favourite councillor were having their weekly meeting in his office. It was Friday morning; her husband worked on Fridays while his wife was at yoga and played around with crafts at the seniors' centre until lunch time. The rest of the councillors never bothered turning up on a Friday so the mayor and the councillor, Mary Moron, as the boys called her, always used his office every Friday to get the most out of their alliance.

As a result of these meetings the councillor tended to agree with everything that the mayor stated or put forward in council and when it came to a vote no matter what the issue, the mayor and the councillor always tended to vote the same way.

Those sounds of joy you would hear coming from the mayor's Friday meeting with his councillor must have been a true indication that they were in harmony with the particular affair that they were working on

On numerous occasions Mrs. Mayor had asked the leading question. 'What do you find to do in city hall every Friday morning? You don't see any of the other councillors around they all have family business to do on a Friday much the same as most of the staff there.'

'How would you know, you are busy drinking coffee with your cronies, talking each other to death?'

Mrs. Mayor, like her husband, was a retired school teacher. She had gone to school where she mixed with children of her own age, gone to university where she mixed with youths of her own age then mixed with children again mentally of her own age as she taught them. This allowed her to become very opinionated as the majority of her students never stood up to her which suited her just fine.

Now having retired and having mixed with children and youths all her life, the real world full of adults seemed a rather baffling place so much so that she spent her time trying to impress and improve her social standing. When her husband made it as a councillor she was determined to impress. However, with her husband now the mayor she was out to make sure that everybody knew who she was. If she wasn't already, she became an over-bearing, arrogant, snob, everybody in the community knew her and stayed well away from her.

Whereas her husband, the mayor, having had a similar up-bringing and career had stumbled and fallen into his new career as a councillor. When the election for the mayoral position became vacant four years later it dawned on him that nobody wanted it, so he went for it and won by acclamation.

As he found out as mayor, it was just like being a teacher, he could act as the top dog as most of the councillors as indeed were the children, were intimidated by the fact that he was the senior person and had that antagonistic approach to other people that bullies do. He found it difficult to look the part in council meetings and at official functions as he wasn't used to dressing up. He looked fashionable in that dishevelled way without knowing it, dressed in his old faithful shirts and creased pants.

'Mrs. what's it told me her husband is the janitor and he said it's easy to clean up on a Friday because there's nobody around. She wanted to know why your office was the only one he cannot clean, he said he can never get in to clean it on a Friday because its always locked.'

This was the last thing he needed. Why didn't he just keep his mouth shut and not engage her in conversation. He was thinking to himself about his golden rules, never put anything in writing and always keep conversations short.

'I always lock my office.'

But she carried on like a popcorn machine.

'He said that his universal key won't work in your lock. He says you must be there or at least someone is there because there are noises'

'What are you talking about now'

'Well, he said he can never get in to clean your office on a Friday because it's always locked.'

'Well, I always lock my office.' he repeated.

On she went, 'He said that his special key won't work in your lock. He says you must be there or someone is because there are noises'

By this time, he was getting frustrated and nervous, he felt sweaty. No wonder she gave him a headache. She's like a bloody parrot on and on. In his mind he thought at least he could strangle a parrot and throw it in the garbage, disposal wouldn't be a problem. Just imagine getting rid of her it would need a piece of heavy equipment.

'What kind of noises?'

'Well like grunting and heavy breathing.'

'Grunting and heavy breathing, his hearing must be going,' said the mayor.

'Well, that's what he said'

One skill he did develop when dealing with school kids was thinking on his feet.

'I go in for a bit of peace and quiet to get caught up on my paperwork. That's the trouble when you have an open-door policy, people actually take advantage of it. I was reading an article about doing two things at once. His juices were beginning to flow and his lying creativity was starting to flow. I will confess I have been taking the chance to do some exercises while at my desk.'

'You are pathetic, why not go to the gym like normal people.'

'Think about it, people will recognize me'

'Who cares, they would say there's our mayor looking after himself. Not like some of the out of shape buffoons on your council. You could set a precedent.'

The mayor was starting to get a bit more excited just wishing that she would shut up.

'You don't get it do you I can't do paperwork while I am walking round the track and people would be bothering me expecting me to be nice to them.'

'I've always said a person in my husband's position should have his own private secretary.'

'Thank goodness I am getting away from her for a few days next week. These out-of-town conferences are great, getting paid to get together, attend a couple of boring presentations and then have a few drinks and nice meals. Amazing what gets paid from property taxes. The most difficult part is finding a nice secluded restaurant where we can have a sponsored dinner.'

Love it she said.

They lay in bed together chatting away about what they would do to the city, they honestly believed that the city was theirs to rule. This authority was never more illustrated than when a senior who had lived in the city for over 70 years had dared criticize the mayor and council on how they were running and or ruining the city. His response was plain and simple.

'If you don't like it pack your bags and leave'

Friday morning came once more and it was while intertwined on his new office sofa with Mary Moron, his hands all over her body, before wandering down her legs.

Somehow this led his mind to wander to legs of the new highway and auxiliary traffic routes.

In order to ease the amount of traffic, especially the heavy-duty stuff, the city built a ring road, but unlike most ring roads this one didn't circle the city.

Typically, the city didn't complete it and what they did build was only one lane each way. It created bottlenecks and thus made trips longer. Therefore, people continued to take the old route through the city.

"Eureka" he yelled

Am I turning you on that much my darling
No, you moron, but I have a great idea, oooh she moaned waiting for his hands to wander a bit more.

As he lay there with Mary on top of him, he started to lecture her. What if we force them on to the ring road by making it so onerous to travel through the city that the swine will be only too grateful to use the ring road.

The thought of his plan revitalized him and the councillor immediately felt the benefit. Not that this revitalization lasted too long, it didn't do much for the councillor either

'Let's get moving and get some dinner,' said the councillor, but the mayor's mind was working in other directions, he was hatching his plan

The mayor leant across the restaurant table and looked in her eyes, the Moron waited with baited breath and smiled.

'Councillor, as head of the traffic committee devise a plan to make traveling on the city roads absolutely hideous.'

The mayor's idea was forced on the council, the slowest traffic flow possible was devised, traffic lights at every intersection, traffic could only go one way at an intersection all the other lanes were held up by lights which were purposely not coordinated. Then the crowning glory; hidden speed traps along the route and photo radar at every intersection just in case anybody managed to get above the speed limit.

To the mayor it was not only a means to an end, but a cash cow, a thing of beauty. He was positive the ring road would be back in business and transport trucks and through traffic going through the city would be a thing of the past.

It was Friday some months later; they got off the mayor's sofa puffing and panting she couldn't understand why they couldn't use a hotel room. "You've got to be kidding, in Mere Folly everybody knows us"

She then suggested they make the thirty-minute drive to the metropolis to the south, but he soon dismissed that idea on the grounds that somebody still might recognize them

'You mean to say that all I am worth to you is ten minutes on a sofa. If I hadn't of complained we would still have been having our ten minutes on a bloody desk. Well, I've had enough of this'

He really couldn't see her point.

'What about if we tell council that the mayor should have a separate apartment.'

'When they ask what for, are you going to tell them that it will be far easier to bonk councillor Moron in private. You really are a door knob.'

'We might as well fess up and tell everybody that we are a couple'

That's the last thing the mayor wanted he was quite happy to have her double his vote or back him up coupled with a bit of nookie when he wanted it. She was dumb enough to suggest it but the mayor laughed when he thought of himself living with her.

Thinking quickly, 'that would be great but what do you think the voters would say'

'Fuck the voters I want you'

Oh no, how do I talk my way out of this gem he thought.

'Well let's chat and figure out how we do it'

'It's easy, I'll go home to Roderick right now and tell the prick.'

That's the last thing the mayor wanted; he was quite happy with his life the way it was. He was still trying to think on his feet and quickly at that, but was struggling for an excuse.

'Do you want to carry on or not'.

He grabbed her wishing he could shut her up.

Without thinking, as if by intuition he thrust his lips on to hers then stuck his tongue in her mouth.

'mmmmm' she sighed …

'He knew he had time ... not much but if he could switch the emphasis to sex she would switch off and give him time to think

It worked.

He got off her and steadied himself from the sofa as she stuck her arm out to steady herself, she swept a phone off the table. Picking it up and almost by instinct and or desire grabbed the phone fumbled for the camera button and took a duo selfie as they lay nude and intertwined on their backs on the floor. Normally, a picture like that would be just two people having sex but, in this case, it was quite clearly the mayor and councillor Moron having sex

Desire took over; she grabbed the phone again and took another selfie of them tangled up on the floor

'Anybody in there?'

'Yes, I am' shouted back the mayor.

'Sorry I'll come back later'

Archie the janitor knew that every Friday morning when he went to clean the mayor's office the door was locked from the inside and he would have to come back, but like most of the staff he couldn't stand the arrogant son of a bitch so he knocked on the door just to piss him off.

As most of the staff by now figured the councillor was not in the locked mayor's office discussing the state of the city

They quickly got dressed, she had a bag in the cupboard with the usual beauty accoutrements in it. The councillor went about tidying herself up then slipped out the office

I don't know why they don't get a bed in there and do it in comfort said Archie to himself from the broom cupboard around the corner

The mayor left the office. Archie it's all yours I will be back in a bit I'm just nipping to get some gas I am literally running on fumes'

'Yes sure' said Archie as he walked in. 'Eh don't you want your phone'

Too late he'd gone

Just then a barking dog sound from came from the phone. Archie picked it up and laughed as he saw it was the mayor's wife. What a shame she didn't phone 15 minutes ago he thought while they were at it. Archie had met the mayor's wife; she would kill him with one lash of her tongue if she knew that she was a barking dog sound on his phone. She left a voice mail telling him that she had finished early and was popping in to see him. Again, he survived by the skin of his teeth. Then she texted him again, Archie was so disappointed that she couldn't catch them at it just the once white he was around to see the fireworks

After reading the text he inadvertently slipped the phone in his pocket and then went on about his duties

Eventually the mayor made it to the gas station in the north end of the city always four or five cents cheaper than anywhere else.

As he drove in, a car was in the bay, an empty bay in front of it. He'd have got all bent out of shape but he saw that there was somebody in the car. However, two minutes later it was still there. By then another a truck had pulled up behind him to join the line and still the car sat there.

The driver of the truck got out, "Has it died?" he asked the mayor

"How am I supposed to know' the mayor said as he followed the other guy to the car.

"I don't fff'n well believe it" he yelled as he banged on the car's window, "she's on her fff'n well phone'

The message got through to her, she panicked, started her car, which was at an angle, knocked a box of bottled water all over the place and took off.

The mayor by now getting really anxious, got in his car, drove over a bunch of littered bottles to the front gas pump. It seemed to take ages to fill up his car. Eventually, he got in his car to drive away when right in front of him sat a Mercedes.

Back up, you dumb bitch, he yelled through his windshield. The woman just sat there in her Mercedes. Again, the guy in the truck was at the mayor's window. 'What the hell is going on now' he shouted. 'Can you believe it bellowed the trucker?'

"Back up you idiot, we will then get out and you can get in"

"You back up she shouted back"

"You really are an idiot," said the mayor.

By then there were two vehicles waiting behind the two vehicles at the pumps.

'We can't back up you clown, back up or I will call the police and have you towed away you dumb idiot."

Then the truck driver joined in. "Get in your car and push her out of the way"

"You touch my car and I will sue you" she screamed

The mayor was getting incredulous, when halleluiah the cavalry, well, a police car rolled up. He had been summoned by the cashier in the gas station office

It didn't take him long to size up the situation and recognizing the mayor he approached the woman and politely asked her to back up her car

"Why", she asked. In her mind she wanted to move her car but was more afraid of losing her dignity. So, the standoff continued. The spectators, there were about twenty of them by now.

"Madam" said the officer, 'You are causing an obstruction and if you don't clear it, I will have no alternative but to arrest you and have your car towed.'

"You'll be hearing from my lawyers" she yelled almost in tears as she backed up her car just missing another one and screeched out of the gas station

"Thank you, officer," said the mayor as he got in his car and screeched out of the gas station

Driving along he was thinking about how he had brought in traffic lights at every junction and to really snarl up the traffic you could only make a turn on a green light. Then to compound his vengeance he had the engineers who programmed the lights ensure that any driver couldn't go through two lights in a row This was not only part of his master plan to get the heavy trucks out of the city and through traffic using the ring road, but also revenge. Payback for the guy who sat on his bumper one day and then sped past him giving him the finger. Then there was the other guy; just because he blocked him in in the down town parking lot he had the nerve to get out of his car and yell at the mayor

'Its about time you clowns at City Hall left some space for citizens of this damn city to be able to park to enable us to do our business or spend our money.'

He was quite right as many people were furious due to the fact that the public parking lot was full of city employees parking for nothing.

'It's about time you clowns realize who pays your salaries and you know what Mr. Mayor you are not just a clown you are an arsehole '

The mayor drove off vowing revenge which in his mind he had now achieved by slowing traffic in the city to a crawl

The city had now become home to a mass of box stores with only two main roads to service them. There were no quality specialty stores. Even downtown which was built to provide authentic, original, inventive, cutesy stores, galleries, restaurants and cafes was composed of offices for doctors, lawyers, accountants and insurance agents. Citizens, visitors and tourists were drawn to these areas by innovative stores, restaurants etc. not office blocks.

The funniest spot was the traffic island and road to nowhere. One councillor got up the mayor's nose in a session one day saying that with the extra traffic lights, it was a nightmare trying to drive by city hall.

Ok said the mayor why don't we take out a set of lights, an idea he had hatched whilst in his favourite position with the chairwoman of the traffic committee.

Councillor Ackroyd was beside himself. 'There is only one lane going around the island yet there are two roads leading to it and what's this road going to the right its going to a dead end. There will be traffic chaos.'

'You were the one who wanted away with the traffic lights, so here it is, the answer,' said the mayor

'Bullshit,' said the councillor, 'this is bullshit you will never get this through.'

With the mayors bullying, favors owing and bribery the new island became reality. The mayor licked his lips at the thought of even more congestion.

On his way back, he nipped home expecting to see his wife. As he walked in the phone went

"Oh, you are home'

'Where are you?'

'On my way to drop in some cookies to your office I tried your mobile but you didn't answer'

Why would she drop in with cookies, that was just not her style? Obviously, the bitch wants to see for herself what is going on as the pangs of guilt crept over him.

Oh shit, it dawned on him that his phone was on his desk. What if she picks it up and opens it up........

'Bring them home then we can have them here'

She said that she had to pop in the library and would give them to Archie and the others and leave some in his desk.

She couldn't find anybody around

At home sweat was beading down the mayor's face. Oh shit, oh shit he thought

'I'll put them in your desk'
'But it's locked'
'I'll get Archie to let me in'
'It's like you don't want me to give your cookies away' she said innocently'

He was beside himself wondering what would happen if she messed with the phone. The mayor was so low tech he didn't even know yet think about a password lock.

The mayor put the phone down and jumped into his car. Off he went at a rate of knots until he hit the first set of lights. Come on come on, he was in the outside lane then just as he got to the lights they changed. Sod it, he went straight through then cut to the inside lane to turn right on to the main road south. He didn't look in his mirror as he would have seen a cop pulling out of Tim Hortons with donuts for the staff at the cop shop

As per his orders, the lights were there to make it difficult for anybody to go through the city without stopping. That didn't bother him he was on a mission just as he got to the next set the they had changed. Zap his pride and joy, the red-light camera got him and the Tim Hortons delivery vehicle stopped right in front of him as well. The cop forgave him the for first infraction as he wanted to get the coffee and donuts to the cop shop but this was too much. He was mad as the cops at the shop would be waiting

He wasn't going to stop, lucky or unlucky for him the red lights ahead were holding up the traffic. The cop, lights flashing weaved his way through the held-up traffic. The mayor wasn't even aware of the cop he was more stressed out as to whether his wife had found his phone

'Who do you think you are Gilles Villeneuve?'
'No, whoever he is, I'm the bloody mayor'

That really upset the cop. His coffee getting cold and this pompous prick swears at him. Right so that gives you special dispensation to go through red lights at excessive speed.

'Listen you jumped up prick I designed this traffic system to slow everybody down and make it difficult for the arse holes like you to get about'

'I'll pretend that I didn't hear that sir as you are rather emotional and would like to get on your way.'.

Indeed, he was but so was the cop as his buddies in the cop shop were waiting for their caffeine fix and donuts

Strange to say the mayor suddenly realised that he had to get back to the city hall and had a complete change of character, 'apologies officer I am due at city Hall on important business.'

I tell you what I am going to give you a big break and let you off with a caution, slow down and behave.'

The cop was actually thinking that the comments about cold coffee would be bad and then he would have to go to court and be a witness in the mayor's court case, it would take up his time doing reports and the eyes of the world would be on him to check to see if he had done everything right. Why bother, life's too short for that crap'

Off he went to deliver the coffee and donuts.

Meanwhile, the mayor was in a race against time, or so he thought. He made it to city hall without further mishaps parked right outside and raced, as best he could, to his office where he expected to meet his wife

It was earie and desolate nobody around. Had his wife found the phone. What was she doing, had she found it and opened it. Had she discovered the selfie. If she had he would be dead.

She would be waiting for him ready to kill him surely for the first time in a couple of hours he was feeling comfortable

The phone wasn't on the desk he even searched the drawers, nothing. He called her at home, the phone answered straight away.

'Where are you?'

'I am in the office, coming home right away dear.'

He knew he shouldn't have said dear it gave the impression that he was guilty of something. She put the phone down

The ride home felt even longer than the one getting there

'Hi', he said half expecting her to confront him with the evidence

'I wanted to talk to you'

'Oh no', a shiver went up his back, he felt numb waiting for the axe to fall

'I forgot to tell you that we are going to the Smiths for dinner tonight. Now I know you don't like them but she is my closest friend.'

Normally, this would be as big a crisis as the mayor would face in his day-to-day autocracy, he would have blurted out 'no bloody way' but he hardly heard what she was saying only that he was safe, for the time being anyway.

There was stunned silence

He was going to agree straight away, anything to keep the peace, but she carried on regardless and asked if he would do it for her sake. Still basking in relief, 'OK, for you' he squeaked out

'Thank you dear, you're a gem'

Again, he didn't pay much attention, his mind was too preoccupied. Now that was strange, he thought as he went into the other room She couldn't have found the phone as he would have been chopped liver he couldn't have missed it as it was right on the desk it would have been the first thing she saw

So where did it go?

Mrs. Mayor was ready for a battle with her husband in case he threw a tantrum over going to the Smiths and getting the answer she wanted that she didn't really notice or feel how easy it had been

The Mayor wandered around, then he thought that he would take the bull by the horns. He asked her if she had seen his phone.

'No'

'Isn't it here?'

All of a sudden, the mayor had become a little more contrite, normally he would have responded with, 'of course it isn't or else I wouldn't be asking would I (you bloody hen)' under his breath

'Did you leave it in your office'

Was she playing games?

'I didn't see it when I was there'

'Try calling it'

'Good idea'

He went to the land line and rang his mobile.

The mobile rang in Archie's jacket pocket which was hanging on the store room chair. The ringing obviously took Archie by surprise. Once he had figured out what was happening and it dawned on him what it was, he grabbed his jacket. He fumbled it out of the inside pocket, nearly dropped it in his haste, juggled it round so that he could look at it. Too late, by the time he was looking at it, it had gone silent. He stared at the phone realising that he had forgotten all about it being in his pocket.

Back at the Mayor's home there was just as much thought going on. On one hand the Mayor was ecstatic that obviously his wife didn't have it or else he would have heard it ring. On the other though, where the hell was it?

'You had better report it stolen and get another one. That's the beauty of being Mayor, I am always telling the ladies that in our position we have many benefits such as in this case not having to pay for our phones'

His first thought was to tell her that she shouldn't be disclosing things like that and that she was a bloody snobby bitch, but now was not the time. He couldn't report it because whoever had it would see the incredibly compromising selfies of him and the councillor if they opened it

Oh shit, what can I do?

Archie was also in a dilemma as he had in his hand the mobile. He would have been in even more of a dilemma if found the incredibly compromising selfie of the Mayor and the councillor, but he was so concerned with what he should do with the phone that he never gave it a thought to examine it. Besides that, Archie didn't have a mobile anyway and hadn't a clue of how to switch it on or even use it.

A well, its not that important, he would give to the mayor next time he saw him and put back in his inside pocket. Hopefully the dumb thing doesn't go off again he thought.

It was one of those summer evenings after a blue-sky day. Archie was on his deck when he smelled the smoke of a fire pit. The boys must be out there; he got a sweater out of the closet and then noticed the phone which he had stuck on the chest of drawers when he hung his jacket up. Funny he thought, why a big wig like him wouldn't be phoning all the time to see if somebody had picked it up. That's why the city administration is a mess with that clown in charge.

He put the phone in his pocket, told his wife he was off for a glass of wine and strode around the corner.

Great minds think alike; Bert was also on his way to the fire pit. It was always a bit of an ad hoc scenario as Kev and Jim lived next door to each other and if doing nothing would light that fire, then see who turned up.

There was no fence between the neighbors instead a swath of beautiful maples went through from east to west. So, there it was the fire pit with the fire spitting away under the maples idyllic

One may ask how one gets a fire permit for a fire pit under the canopy of a maple tree. Simple; the beauty of a glass of Gareth and Roger's pear, apple and grape wine and a few extra bottles for the fire department's inspection unit to go home with

There they were, the boys enjoying a convivial glass of wine relaxing by the fire pit with the sparks shooting through the leaves into the darkening sky on a beautiful warm evening

What about those pricks in City hall did you read the paper today, now they are sending caustic e mails to each other. Even though you think it why would you put derogatory stuff like that in writing. How does a city like ours jam-packed in the main with mature intelligent people have to put up with a council full of vengeful idiots?

That's easy, quality people don't want to go through the bullshit of getting elected, having to work with union mentality government employees, having to suck up to the media and not being allowed a private life. So, we end up with idiots on council who probably couldn't get a job elsewhere, it's the same with the provincial MLA's, most of them are ego maniacs so they engineer themselves a position where they can laud it over people. It's a position that only few want

Just then Archie who was also retired but worked part time at City Hall for something to do, waiting for his glass to be refreshed pulled out the phone. What should I do with this?

'Well, if you don't know now ………'

'No, you plonker, guess who this belongs to'

For once stunned silence.

'You mean you have actually gone into the modern world and got yourself a phone'

'No way, why do I need one, the little lady would be chasing me all the time. The less she can keep tabs on me the better I like.' laughed Archie

'No, himself'

'Himself?'

'Yes, himself, the Mayor'

'You are kidding, how did you come by that?"

Archie told them the story

'I wonder if we can figure out his password,' said Bert. '

Tom took the phone, 'let's take a look. Oh, great it's dead as a dodo.

'Hold on.' Kev nipped to his house and came back with an extension cord and a phone cable. 'Same as mine' as he connected it to the phone.

'You have to be kidding, what idiot wouldn't password protect his phone'

'I rest my case,' said Kev

Let's have a look, the boys shouted in unison, as they couldn't wait to have a look at the Mayor's phone. All except Archie, by then he had had enough of the dam thing. You guys get it back to the Mayor, I'm off home I must be up early in the morning and besides that I don't want to be involved with the mayor he's a slime ball.

As soon as Archie had disappeared, they took a look at the phone. Wow look at this said Jim as they viewed the photos.

'That's the Mayor and Mary Moron.'

'We have to be careful. Are you thinking what I am thinking.' Said Tom

'Yes, but bribery is illegal,' alleged Jim

'Yes, but there is bribery and bribery. I would rather call it a means to an end with a guarantee. Think about it: why don't we do a test run and see what happens, what have we got to lose?' asked Tom

'Our freedom' said Bert, 'got it,' he carried on, the wine was really getting the creative juices working, 'it's the neighborhood party next Saturday, will the Mayor be there?'

'I doubt it, it's not an election year he only comes the year of an election.'

'That's a blow, we really need him there.'

'Let's take another glance at that phone, boy is that an ugly photograph, I mean those two aren't exactly your actual things of beauty are they.'

'You got it again' yelled Jim, things of beauty, birds, crows, Percy.

'Where did that come from,' asked Kev in his usual sarcastic manner.

'Probably too much wine' he added rhetorically.

'Percy knows the mayor, let's get him to ask him to come.'

'Come on, grow up,' said Tom, 'the Mayor isn't going to pop in to our neighbourhood party unless there is something in it for him. Hence why he only comes in election years.'

Jim jumped in, 'Well let's make it worth his while, let's tell him we want to make a presentation to him.'

'Wonderful, what are we going to present him with' said Kev'/.

'Does it matter, in fact we are not going to present him with anything, why would anybody give that bozo anything, but he's not to know that.'

'He's going to be pretty upset and say we got him here under false pretense, isn't he?'

'That's up to him, if he does, we will tell him he got it wrong, we'll tell him we thought he would be happy to mix with the residents of Mere Folly. We do want him here so that we can make a presentation,'

"I don't get it" said Kev

'There is a difference between presenting something to someone md making a presentation to someone,' said Jim. 'We are not going to present him with anything. We are going to make him a presentation on the vineyard, we will take him to the Cote de Mere Folly and explain the plan and get his response'

'What if he doesn't like it which will probably be the case'

'Then we go to plan B'

'Which is?'

'Pure unadulterated blackmail' said Bert smiling as he took the phone, 'OK let's take a look and see what else is in here.'

A few miles away the Mayor was not having such a convivial evening. Firstly, he was having to put up with the Smiths and be charming as his wife insisted. There is no way our mayor knew what charming was even if it hit him on the head

Charley Smith was a building contractor. After years on building sites, he had built his company to the level where he spent most of his time in the office or developing connections. Over the years of building relationships in restaurants and bars, the waistline had started to expand, because a balanced meal to Charley was two pints of beer and two pizzas. Over the past few years, he had been trying to get the mayor to give him the odd city job or two. He didn't fabricate the fact of why he was there. If it meant having to put up with Mrs. Mayor and her stuck-up disdainful snobbery then so be it. While the two wives chatted away oblivious and too dim to understand Charley's motives, Charley was working on the mayor.

The mayor had Charley do his bathroom and Charley had not billed him for it. Most city officials would obviously be concerned over the ulterior motive if they didn't get a bill.

Not our mayor he was thrilled at the time but of course Charley now had something on him and kept pressing him for city jobs. They were good for each other; the mayor would get work done around the house and Charley would get small jobs for the City

While he was straining every sinew to be "charming" he had the nagging thought of where his phone was and did anybody have it. Surely, if somebody had found it they would have been in touch by now What if I give it one more try to see if there is an answer

While Charley went to the washroom, the women clucked at each other. The mayor snook up the stairs to ring his mobile. The beer was clicking his bravado into a higher gear

The boys were about to further check the phone out when it rang. On the screen appeared "HOME"

'Should we answer it?', 'no' said Kev. They let it ring out its time. 'If we had answered it we would have had to make a comment and talk, which we are not prepared for'

'Yes, good thinking' said Jim 'let the bastard stew. We know that he is concerned, he is stewing, he doesn't know who has it.'

Theoretically, anyone with some common sense would realise that the phone is dead or will soon die,' suggested Tom. 'This was probably his final shot, to my mind he will start to relax now thinking and hoping that the phone fell behind a cupboard or into a crevice. The key is that we will have the element of surprise when we hopefully meet with him next Saturday '

The mayor was somewhat relieved, he was now convinced that nobody had his phone He went back and chit chatted with Charley for the rest of the evening as his charm was exemplified by the amount of beer consumed, however his logic and thought process wasn't. As they parted, he mentioned to Charley that some additional work could be coming his way and that they both would receive "mutual benefits" from it.

Afterwards Mrs. Mayor was flitting around full of the joys of spring praising him on how charming he was and how pleased Mrs. Smith was that the two of them had got on so well. The Mayor though muttered under his breath if he was going to have to put up with that pleb he might as well get something out of it.

Then the boys, also full of the joys of spring staggered back to their respective abodes with the feelings that their project and plan was a little more than a dream. Would they have the guts to proceed and bring their dreams and fantasies to reality. The realization of what they were about to do would come in the morning when they were sober.

Next morning each of them was waiting for somebody to make a move. None of them had slept much as a result of the information and thoughts going through their heads. The wine didn't help either Kev decided to take his garbage bin out.

'What's got into you' asked his wife somewhat sarcastically

'I thought I might as well get it done, are you feeling ok?'

'I'm fine'

'Pity' he whispered

Tom and Bert appeared; both had been hiding in their respective garages waiting for some activity.

'Have you seen Jim?' just then Jim rode up on his bike, he couldn't sleep so he got up early and went for a ride

'I've been thinking about last click after click and feel the same way I did last night let's go for it. A chance like this will never happen again.'

The others were just as enthusiastic; the collective comments were to the effect that if we don't do it we will be sat having a Friday beer in 5 years chatting about the same old things. All that money we have wasted on the lottery. What if we had taken advantage of the mayor's phone. What if we had built the vineyard. That's providing that we are here in five years. What's the worst thing that can happen. Five senile seniors who didn't know what they were doing. We'll get a rap on the knuckles and a bit of bad press in the paper.

'We are right' said Tom 'and bringing up the paper, every time you read the odd bit of news amongst the adverts and especially the letters to the editor you really wonder about the governance of this city. Then there is the crap that goes on and comes out of that Council. Gentlemen, the door's wide open not only to go and do something to curtail this garbage but also have some fun with these clowns.'

They shook hands

All of a sudden as if by radar four women appeared.

'What are you layabouts up to now' said Bert's wife.

Bert had had enough, 'Discussing our vineyard,'

'Oh no not again,' You guys are pathetic. All you do is talk, talk and talk. If you are that keen, why don't you take the bull by the horns and do something about it'

There was no comment, only a smile as the boys went their various ways

I suppose when one looks at a small place like Mere Folly, especially on a Saturday morning, what is there to do especially in the winter. One can tidy up the house, go shopping, DIY or watch the grand kids play hockey

'Jim's got the best idea,' said Bert, he's a genius. Who else would go to Phoenix for the winter and leave their wife up here to work.'

However, the few months that are summer, Saturday mornings are what we all look forward to blue sky the chance to play or watch sport, go for walks shop, the farmers market, have coffee at an open-air cafe or just sit on your deck. You can understand our delightful Mayor saying if you don't like it move

Of course, when he said it, it wasn't in this context

The residents of Mere Folly are proud of their city. In a lot of cases their forefathers have lived there for generations and together with newer residents have together built a city that has attracted even newer, newer residents

Having helped build the city and being proud of it they feel entitled to comment on its condition and progress as and when the time might arise. Regardless of what the Mayor tends to think we still live in a democracy and whether he agrees or not with these comments he has to realise that he is an elected official not a bloody dictator.

Perfect day for the neighbourhood party which as usual would take place in the park on top of the hill

Bert was walking up the street and crossed the road to chat with Kev. It's a good day for it. Well, the odds for sunshine today are good, I was just chatting with Percy and if anybody would know, he would.

Without Percy the event would never happen, it's a typical community event that nobody likes to organise let alone compere. He'd been the life and sole of the party ever since it started, mind you, Percy was one of the few people who actually thought the Mayor was doing a good job.

Percy was a quiet sole and met the mayor at a community function. He was thrilled that he had actually spoken to the him, the mayor literally brushed past him and offered a word as he looked down on him in his usual condescending way. Every year Percy would send the mayor a hand-written invite and every year bar one the mayor would ignore it. This year though, the mayor had responded, he was thrilled as he told Mrs. Mayor that there was going to be a presentation to him. Mrs. Mayor spent the next week telling everybody she spoke to that the people of Mere Folly were so grateful to her husband that they were going to be making a presentation to him.

The boys were trying to figure out how they were going to approach this, 'presentation'. Well, as we discussed, drag him down to the hill and put it to him. If he agrees, which he won't, then we will go to plan B the heavy artillery

Tom wasn't so sure, 'remember he's a bully and has spent his whole life forcing other people to do what he wants, if we push him into a corner, you never know what he might do'

'You know what a bullied person does;' gives in because they are afraid of the consequences.'

'I agree said Kev it is now or never we have to go for it and stand up against this bloody tyrant.'

They were in full agreement, 'it will be one bully less, nobody will feel sorry for him.' They despised the guy and were really looking forward to clamping down on his pleasures and ego. Then they started second guessing themselves; suppose they were to get him ousted; he would be reduced to just a normal citizen. His ego would be compromised, reprobates like him have a habit of turning up when and where you least expect them and in positions that affect you. No, the plan was to make sure that he stayed on as Mayor. Let him have his dirty weekends and play around with the taxpayer's money as long as the boys had the dirt on him so that they could control him and literally run the city through him. The citizens of Mere Folly would benefit more so than if the Mayor was left to his own devices to run the city.

'Remember', said Bert, 'in future no phone calls or even e mails to discuss matters, we trust no one. Personally, I am looking forward to a glass of APG wine tonight to celebrate. See you later and good luck gentlemen'

4.

'A bunch of new people here this year' said Jim, looking around. There were also a lot more younger kids which showed signs of the gradual change in the neighbourhood demographics.

Tom took a hamburger from Tony who every year hauled his barbecue up the hill and cooked the city provided hot dogs and hamburgers. Just then there was a stir amongst the patrons as a cyclist arrived, helmet and all. This was the mayor's new image the eco guy.

The boys smiled at each other, they found it hard to believe that he was the guy in the selfie.

Percy wandered over to welcome him, people stopped in mid conversation. "It's the mayor it's the mayor what's he doing here?'

'Didn't know he could ride a bike, probably borrowed it from the city lost and found to create the impression.' He was right, the helmet didn't fit. 'I bet it's not his' said Kev.

People were shell shocked that the mayor had turned up in a non-election year. Must have been promised something smirked Tom.

'All right, will you guys be nice for once in your lives" said Tom's wife

Percy started his speech. Always down to the point and eloquent with it, he introduced and thanked the mayor for attending and the city for providing the food.

From where the boys were stood somebody yelled, 'Have you got your dates mixed up, Mr. Mayor, it's not an election year.'

The mayor responded with a kind of smile through his teeth muttering under his breath "arsehole".

Percy and the Mayor were chatting away with the mayor getting agitated, wondering how long it would be before they made the presentation as he wanted to get away from these bimbos. As far as he was concerned it was a complete waste of time. He was wishing he hadn't bothered and more so ke was annoyed at himself for not telling them to drop his gift to City Hall

The boy's circled Percy asking if they could borrow the mayor for a minute. 'We have something here that we feel will really interest him,' said Jim.

The Mayor appeared quite astonished, the presentation at last, as the boys ushered him away to the top of the hill. However, it wasn't to be the type of presentation he was expecting.

The wives saw what was happening and gathered together. 'I don't believe it, said Jim's wife, 'I can't believe that they are going to go ahead and talk to the mayor about the vineyard,' they just cracked up laughing 'they've got no chance.'

Of course, they hadn't got a clue about plan B, the phone and the selfies.

The boys had been married long enough and thus were experts at only disclosing what they wanted their wives to know
'We have an idea that will benefit you and the City, especially with an election coming up in a year or so,' said Tom tongue in cheek.

They took him down the path to the hill or Côte, to be precise, as they were now going in to the wine business. 'Let us show you what we have in mind Mr. Mayor,' who still believed that a presentation was in the offing At the top of the cote Jim pointed the mayor to the south west. They were overlooking the river some half a mile away with the valley surrounding it.

'Beautiful eh Mr. Mayor' added Bert.

'So, this is what you have brought me here for, a geography lesson. Where's my present?'

This is it said Bert, a beautiful view of Mere Folly.

The mayor had run out of patience, 'This is it. This is it, you've got to be joking you pricks. I am going to get my bike'

'Your bike,' Kev couldn't resist it

Ignoring the mayor's s comments, they started the presentation.

'The soil isn't that good it just about supports this motley grass which the city looks after. Mr. Mayor what else could be grown here besides grass?'

'I really don't give a shit'

'Grapes your highness' continued Tom

Bollocks to you as well, you dipstick

'No' said Kev, 'you obviously don't get it, this is the perfect spot for growing grapes.

'You guys must be nuts. Who cares about growing grapes why don't you join the gardening club. By the way, who is going to pay for this disaster'

'Obviously the city' said Tom very seriously.

'I told you; you are all nuts I've had enough'

'Mr. Mayor, the city has lots of little parcels of land dotted around the city, surely, they can be put to good use.'

'I told you that I am not interested, but if you want to apply to the City you can waste your time, I will make sure your application goes nowhere.'

'Why?' asked Tom, appearing to be disappointed.

It's bloody obvious, we haven't got the money and there are too many of these people around who see Mere Folly as an artsy fartsy place. This city will be a place where businesses like lawyers, doctors, dentists, realtors can build offices and pay taxes. The worst thing we ever did was bring in the farmers market the sooner that is moved to the outskirts the better.

'I guess that's a no.' grinned Tom. 'So, we as citizens can't approach you about important matters and concerns, we may have.'

'You know what, you people are, you are a waste of time. What do you know about running anything let alone a city. It's about time that you all realized that it is my city and I will run it how I want to run it.'

'That's priceless, said Kev 'coming from you a failed school teacher.'

As if by divine intervention a mobile rang, it was a familiar barking dog tone.'

Tom pulled out the phone, looked at it and showed the screen to the mayor

'It's your wife,'

All of a sudden, the mayor's bravado had gone down the toilet. It was replaced by a schoolboy, angry at being found with a cigarette in his hand in the school toilets

'I know that you prick, so that's where my phone ended up, you stole it. Why didn't you turn it in.'

'Well normally we would but in this case, we found some of the content very interesting.'

That's theft I am going right now, I'm going straight to the police.; The mayor was getting flustered by the second. He made a stab for the phone that Tom was holding

'You don't think that we would come here without backing up the information on it up do you'

'I'll go to the police and tell them you stole it.'

'Here's your chance' said Jim, as who should come up the pathway on their bikes but two of Canada's finest.

'Hi gentlemen are you part of the neighbourhood party? we are just on our way to meet and greet.'

'That's great' said Tom, 'there are lots of kids especially who would like to meet you, thanks for coming'

'Good day gentlemen and you Mr. Mayor, see you in a bit'

This was the moment that they knew that they were in control. The look on the mayor's face was one of fear, his eyes told the story he couldn't even open his mouth. He was getting bitter and twisted by the minute, he knew that there was no way he could say or do anything as long as that phone was still alive and in their hands.

'We admit that we really haven't gone through your phone in great detail as yet but enough to know that we can work with you or against you. Together we can get you re-elected; without us you have no chance.

Bert loved negotiating, he called a spade a shovel, but the boys were still surprised when he suddenly tore into the mayor. In essence he was fed up as it appeared that the mayor wasn't taking this seriously enough

'Wait till your wife and then your lady councillor friend hear about this and then wait till Mrs. Mayor hears about your out of towners which she doesn't get to go to. Imagine in the newspaper, a letter to the editor asking why on every occasion that there has been a vote, Mary Moron has voted with you.

Than a week or so later a rumour starts circulating about you and her and what you do on a Friday morning.' Bert was on a roll.

'You bastards'

'That's better Mr. Mayor, now we know that you care and you know what, we are deadly serious,' said Bert. 'You really put your foot in your mouth earlier when you said that we knew nothing about business. You are going to find out that we know a hell of a lot more than you ever imagined. We are getting on in life, not many years left. Actually, about this much.' He showed a gap between his thumb and index finger and winked at Jim who cracked up.

The other day they were discussing life span as a comparison to the length of a ruler. Ever since then the in joke had been Jim holding out his thumb and index finger when asked how much time any one of them had eft on earth, he would respond by using the gap and saying "about this much"

Bert carried on, 'Mr. Mayor, you are a bloody bully, guess what, you are about to feel what its like to be bullied.' You've been bullying people for years Your reputation goes before you; everybody knows that you are a prize bully. There's one thing you are going to learn you prick, bullying isn't going to work on us. Remember this, we are in this for us, not you. We are not out to ruin or spoil your life or the rest of your life Mr. Mayor. You can resent us and fight back, you can try to get rid of us but remember the data is protected, only one of us has to be compromised and data will be released.'

'Heh it's just like Wikileaks,' added Jim

The mayor was so dumbfounded by Bert's broadside he was too upset to say anything'

Just when the Mayor thought that Bert had finished, he started up again. 'Think very carefully about what we have said, we will pop into city hall Monday morning at 10 to meet with you to get the project moving.'

'But I have meetings Monday morning'

'You weren't listening, were you? cancel them,' ordered Kev

'You've got to be kidding',

'It hasn't stopped you canceling other meetings when you wanted a bit of nookie has it. Think about what would have happened if somebody unscrupulous had of got hold of your phone'. Bert smiled, "I feel better now" he smirked

'You had better go and bid a farewell to Percy and the people in the park,' said Kev.

'I am off' the mayor said 'they can go to hell.'

Bert said quite quietly, 'Mr. Mayor you are missing the point.'

The mayor got the point, and even though he felt nauseous going back up the path, went and did as he was told even though he hated every single minute of it. As soon as he could he left on his bike and rode it to where he had left his truck about 500 yards away, dumped it in the back and drove away

I suppose the mayor loved your idea and can't wait to get started' said Tom's wife.

'Yes dear, in the end he got the message and was quite receptive; we are confident that he will support us going forward'

There was stunned silence, she presumed he was being his usual sarcastic self.

'Where are you off to now'

'Across the road, the fire smells like it's going'

They toasted with the clink of the various containers

'Gentlemen, to the new Mayor of Mere Folly, our puppet on a string'

On his drive home, the mayor was seething, seeking revenge, but how? he couldn't mention anything or tell anybody. He walked into his house.

'How was it,' said Mrs. Mayor wondering what her husband had been presented with.

'The usual crap' he said 'I should have sent somebody else.'

'Yes dear, but you've got to look to the future and the next election. You know how much they all love to see you.' Again, Mrs. Mayor was so besotted with her title that there was no way she would let him relinquish it. She was so pitiful and out of touch that she actually thought that the people of Mere Folly actually liked him

'By the way, has your phone turned up.'

'Not yet.'

Oh dear, I wonder who could have it'

Then he had a brain wave. He was never going to get it back, but at least he knew who had it. So, on Monday he would tell her that he had found his phone behind his credenza. It must have fallen off and broke, he would tell her. It would get her off his back. All of a sudden, he was thinking that the new scenario wasn't that bad. It could have been worse some slime ball could have found his phone. At least four old guys found it and no matter what charade they play he was adamant that he would make them pay

5.

Nine thirty he was in his office getting his staff cancelling meetings for the day. Then he was on the phone telling his wife he had found his phone but it was broken and would be replaced.

'A blessing,' said his wife, 'what would have happened if it had got into the hands of an unscrupulous person?'

The mayor sighed

Ten a.m., the boys strode straight through the reception area and into the mayor's office.

'Mr. Mayor, it is such a beautiful morning let's go for a walk by the river and get some fresh air.'

Bewildered, the Mayor got out of his chair, followed on like a puppy through the back door and on to the river pathway.

As the river flowed through the city, it was about twenty yards wide. City hall backed on to it with concrete paths either side following the river right through the City. It really was quite a pretty little valley, but spoilt by the weeds and vegetation that congested the waterway

'What do you think of our proposal Mr. Mayor' said Bert abruptly

'Proposal, you didn't propose anything, I have no option have I'

'No'

The Mayor's mind was racing. He was sensible enough though to realize that he still had options. He could fight them or go along with them. Going along with them would give him time to figure out what to do next. He would hang in and was confident that sooner or later these cretins would slip up and allow him to get rid of the noose around his neck. In his mind he was dealing with four down at heel seniors who had struck lucky and were milking the situation for what it was worth until either ran out of fuel or got bored.

What he didn't know and realize was that the four reprobates were not inexperienced in the ways of the world. Each one of the had substantially more business experience than a guy who had mixed with kids most of his life as a pretty abject teacher. Two had successfully run their own companies and the other two had senior management experience in both north America and Europe.

Of course, it wouldn't occur to the Mayor to do any due diligence to check out who he was dealing with. Common sense doesn't appear to be a prerequisite for the Mayor's job in Mere Folly

OK to business; firstly, the phone

Well, I have come up with something ingenious said the mayor. I have told my wife that it must have fallen behind the credenza and broke and that I would have to get a new one

'Good thinking' said Jim, 'but we can go a stage further. We have got your old phone here with a new case on it so that your wife will think it's new but all your info has been retained addresses etc. etc.'

The mayor actually smiled. This might not be so bad after all he thought

Of course, what they hadn't told him was that a friend of Kev's had been working on the phone so that they had everything backed up and that they could monitor every call, message, text that the mayor made going forward.

'Ok on to our vineyard,' said Tom. 'What needs to be done from a bureaucratic perspective? In other words, we know that anything from City Hall is far from automatic.'

'Leave it to me said the mayor, by the way how do I get hold of you?'

That was something the boys hadn't thought of. We will get back to you on that one, we will be in touch later.'

Off he went

'Obviously, we can't trust him and we didn't want to tell him that we are monitoring his phone.'

Just then the mayor's dummy phone started ringing.

'Hello lovely, where have you been. Didn't hear from you over the weekend and then you cancelled meetings'

They chatted for a bit but it was rather hectic trying to figure out what to tell her and what not to tell her. He was good at lying, after all he had spent most of his married life lying to his wife. Now he was carrying on his talent with his girl-friend. Although many times he had thought to himself how peaceful and non stressful it would be if he didn't have any of this crap. One day. One day. His immediate decision was to tell her nothing, trust nobody

He went on to tell her the edited version of his phone saga and the inquisition from his wife and how he wanted to be with her but couldn't. That really spoilt his weekend he gushed. However, everything was sorted now and he could concentrate on her.

'What are you doing this afternoon?'

'Nothing my precious, my husband won't be home till much later.'

'Should I pop round to discuss our campaigns for re-election'

'Ooooh.'

The boys cracked up on hearing this.

They decided to give him a list of what they wanted doing to the hill so that he the Mayor could discuss with the councillor later.

That evening, the boys developed their list and mini plan, they were well prepared to meet with the mayor and really get the ball rolling

Bert phoned the mayor, 'We need to meet over lunch later.'

'I don't know if I have time', said the agitated mayor.

'Mr. Mayor, we are not asking you if you want to have lunch, we are telling you that we will meet you for lunch later.

He wasn't used to being dictated to. Normally when he fought back people backed away and he got his way

'You have to eat, so do we, we can use that expense account of yours.'

'I have meetings'

'You always have meetings; tell her you are too tired'

The mayor hung up on Bert.

'The bastard hung up on me,' laughed Bert'.

'Surprise, surprise,' mocked Tom

On the third try by Bert the mayor finally answered.

'Where' said a reticent mayor

'Chat at 11.30'

6.

They were the only people in the restaurant and after the pleasantries the five of them ordered and got down to business.

'We feel that as long as you don't do anything stupid and we don't disclose any of what we know about you, you are a shoe in for another four years as mayor. Right?'

'OK' acknowledged the mayor

'We feel that to enhance your campaign you should announce that there are a number of small parcels of city owned land around the city which will be donated to the various communities surrounding them'

'What about land owned by developers etc.?'

'Good question'

'They will be asked to donate a portion to the community with the city managing it.'

'What if they won't', asked the mayor

'Another good question'

'Then there would be a certain amount of public consternation from bad publicity. Then there would be absolutely no co-operation from the city administration going forward.'

'That's blackmail' appealed the mayor

'That's nice coming from you,' said Kev

'Of course, the first project which, if anyone asks, will be a trial one, the Cote de Mere Folly'

'Don't bother taking notes,' directed Tom, 'we have an executive summary for you so that you get everything correct and don't screw this up. Firstly, we have set up a numbered company into which will be transferred the parcel of land. Then we need a meeting with your people responsible for this project. As we said it's all in the summary'.

'We are going a bit quick aren't we,' said an exasperated mayor

'Of course, we have to,' said Kev. 'We are getting on in years and we don't know what's left of the tape. Of course, with some of the things you have been getting up to you might even be impeached. This has to be completed this fall. 'Give us a call tomorrow with an update'

The mayor didn't really enjoy his lunch, he had never experienced anything quite like this, especially as he had to pick up the tab.

'I've got to go'

'Give our regards to councillor Mary.'

The mayor looked back, no they can't, can they?

'Boy is this fun,' said Jim

'What are you guys up to, dining with the Mayor' said Charley, putting cappuccinos on the table. The aroma of sambuca in the hot coffee relaxed everybody.

'That's interesting, said Bert,

'What is?'

'Charley taking boxes out of the restaurant, he's actually working'.

Kev, turned around; 'where?

'Oh, he's gone outside,' said Bert. 'Wait on, he's back',

A few seconds later out he went with another box.

'Seems a bit strange to me,' said Kev, 'normally he'd be bringing boxes in'.

'Perhaps its delivery or take away,' said Tom

'No take away would go through the front door and let's face it Charley isn't your normal delivery driver'.

'Yeah strange,' said Kev

'Are you the new delivery driver?' Bert asked Charley.

He looked back, puzzled at Bert's question

'Oh, the boxes, just doing a bit of tidying I'll take that stuff to the recyclers in the morning'

By the way do you guys need any seafood, lasagna or other stuff, friend's pricing, our cost plus 10%.

'Sure', said Bert, half in jest, 'what have you got, have you got a pricelist'.

Hold on' said Charley and back he came with a pad and paper.

'OK here we go' as he wrote out a list with weights and prices.

The boys suddenly realized that Charley was serious and the chance to pick something up cheap was too good to miss. The prices were quite remarkable.

'How do get away with these prices?' asked Jim.

'As an owner I can look after my friends and make 10%', bullshitted Charley.

'Well,' said Bert 'let's see, well I'll have five pounds of this a couple of these. When he had finished the others took it in turn to place their orders.

'How about next Tuesday, with the cash said Charley? 10 a.m. at the back to load into your cars, it will be ready.'

'Just a minute.'

He then came back from the bar with a bottle of wine.

'By the way we also managed to get this job lot, a special deal on this rather beautiful Amarone. You should try this wine guys. We got it for $129 sells in the liquor store for over $180.'

'Open one up so that we can try it,' said Tom, 'how do we know it's worth that much? $129 for a bottle of wine is way out of our league.'

'Tell you what we can all chip in $25 and we can share the bottle' said Charley.

'No, I have a better idea,' said Bert, 'you give us a taste to celebrate doing business with you.'

'You lot are heathens and crooks,' he said taking his bottle with him.

'Wait a minute' said Tom, as he got out his iPhone and googled the wine.

'What year was it?

'2011' said Bert.

'$86' said Tom.

'Piss off,' said Bert.

'Straight up look.'

'The bloody crook' said Kev, 'with friends like that you don't need enemies'

'Although' said Tom, 'you know, this could be our new office and grocery store as it is so close to our homes and City Hall. Obviously. he's on the make while he can, but we are just a bunch of gullible seniors trying to make ends meet.'

Tuesday morning, the boys picked up their orders and placed new ones for the following Tuesday.

The mayor parked in an office parking lot put his hat on as a disguise and strolled over to the solace of his local mistress.

'I have missed you,' she said as they kissed and made their way up the stairs.

Half an hour later as they were still breathing heavily the mayor sat bolt upright in bed. Sex was over, his mind switched to the matters at hand. I had better read the summary he thought.

'Relax' she said he's away for a couple of days, you should stay the night

'It's not that' he said, 'I have a project I want to push through which will help with my re-election campaign and perhaps yours when you support it.'

'Of course,' she said nibbling at his ear and running her hand down his thigh.

'I'll get the paperwork we can read it together,' once in a day was as much as he could handle

They read through the executive summary

'This is good' she said, 'and the summary.'

The boys wouldn't have expected the summary to be read by the mayor and a councillor in the nude. Whatever it takes I suppose.

They read on. "The hill faces south which will provide warmer nighttime temperatures and it will drain better. The soil isn't that good but with the sparse grass taken off it and a thin layer of compost spread on it, it will develop its own terroir with good physical texture. The soil will be lighter, which will hopefully leave the grapes with a higher sugar content which is amenable to the type of wine we are going to produce."

'Bloody hell they even want a sprinkler system.'

Then he realized that he had no option. 'Good idea though. So, what do you think?'

'I like it' she replied. 'Anything to help you get re-elected. You had better get on it'

So, there was the mayor sending emails, making phone calls, confirming meetings in the nude.

You are to meet with the project manager for the Vineyard project at 2 pm room B second floor city hall.

'Well done Mr. Mayor,' e mailed Tom, 'we are pleased at the progress'

Of course, they could see all the mayor's e mails going backwards and forwards anyway.

The mayor smiled smugly, this might not be too bad, he thought at least he could get some publicity for his campaign for nothing, get re-elected, then sort out these idiots out and get rid of them

The boys trooped into room B at 2 pm.

'Good afternoon,' they said, 'as they shook hands introduced themselves and sat down.

'Right' said Tom, 'as the project manager we anticipate that you will chair the meetings and keep matters moving.'

The project manager was a little bemused as he sat with these four gentlemen who he suddenly realized had been this route before.

'I tell you what' said Kev, 'you probably have lots of questions. Why don't we nip down to Chat and discuss the project over a beer?'

'Where?' said the project manager, 'the new place with the little name, Chat, we'll explain later. '

Over the years the 4 guys had learnt that very early in a meeting, especially with bureaucrats you can tell the people that you will enjoy working with, who want to get things done and the others who don't because it means work for them

This project manager, as they discovered over a couple of beers will help and get this project done.

'I am beginning to get the message' he said feeling more relaxed by the minute. 'Listen guys I will be straight up with you; you honestly think that you can get a project like this through city hall and actually get it finished? Firstly, what's left of the original staff are scared stiff for their jobs they have talent but are not allowed to use it.
Secondly, the mayor just goes out and hires those who will do everything he says. Thirdly, that's why most projects are managed by outside contractors who in turn look after the Mayor. Then of course they hire the sub-contractors to do the work who look after them and of course the Mayor'

'How does the mayor go about getting projects like this through council and then get funding for them?'

'Oh, that's easy, he just does it. It's almost as if he has a bottomless pit. The council does a budget, but once set up it just becomes a pile of money for the mayor to use as he sees fit. I mean look at the state of the roads and snow clearing'
'Take snow clearing and the money thrown at it. Where did it go? I mean we had no snow last year?'

The message was beginning to gel with the boys

'Let's get cracking on the Vineyard' said Bert, 'this bureaucracy is driving me nuts.'

The project manager was still trying to understand why he was working under the direction of these four guys as per direct instructions from the mayor. They seemed quite different to the usual fools that he was told to work with. It really didn't matter though, he'd had enough, he had a job offer in the pipe so he might as well go for the ride. If these guys were genuine, great, if not and they were a bunch of pricks like the mayor and his cronies then he would be able to get out of there anyway. Yet he still couldn't come to terms with the whole scenario. He wondered whose side they were really on. Taking him for a beer, is that a new approach. Did it come from the Mayor, it wouldn't surprise him, that arsehole would try anything?

'Ok let's get going.' said the project manager. How many vines will there be and where are you getting them from, that could be expensive, especially if they don't take'

'Ha ha,' said Tom, 'many years ago there must have been vines on the hillsides here facing south west overlooking the river. Over the years these hillsides have been developed but fortunately some vines have survived. Believe it or not it's fate, we each have a some in our gardens, they are heirlooms we will use them.

Jim has a friend who has about three hundred on his land which we can have. They produce beautiful grapes year after year, they are a mess, he keeps threatening to clear the land. All we have to do is do it for him. If we space at eight feet between plants and twelve feet between rows we will have enough for our vineyard.'

'Hold on a minute said the project manager, let me make notes. That's the spacing, got that, what about the depth.'

'Can you get a back hoe and dig rows about three feet deep, we should be planting the vines about eighteen inches deep'.

'But you want sprinklers.'

'Yes, but you can lay them once you have the vine trenches in place'

'Perfect, tomorrow I will get everything organised' the project manager said in a controlled way. 'I know this is a tricky one,' he said awkwardly, 'but I have a comfort zone working with you guys, can you get me an e-mail from the mayor stating that I actually report to you.?'

'It will be done,' said Tom.

The quick response absolutely shocked the project manager now he really knew who was pulling the strings. This gave the him a certain amount of confidence,

'Ok, just one more question, how did you manage to be in a position to dictate to the mayor like this, have you got dirty photos of him'

'How did you guess,' said Jim chuckling.

Kev was worried, 'aren't we are going to have to learn as much as we can about growing grapes.'

'Hold on' said Bert, 'remember our philosophy, why do things yourself when you can get experts to do them better. Gareth and Roger down the road have been making apple and pear wine for years lets have words, they can be our winemakers.'

'The aim is to grow them, harvest them and produce Cote de Mere Folly. Then we are going to sell it as a novelty, it won't be Premier Cru, but it might improve as we go on and what's more, with the mayor's help, the expenses will be kept to a minimum.'

It didn't take long before the vineyard venture became the topic of conversation, headlines in the local newspaper and the mayor milking the diversification for all its worth as he churned out the campaign rhetoric on the way the City was making use of idle land.

The mayor was visiting the boys to take a look at how the vineyard was doing. They introduced him to Gareth.

'Mr. Mayor do you fancy a glass of wine, let's get Roger and discuss the wine making'

He was beginning to feel more comfortable in the presence of the boys. In fact, in his own mind he was beginning to feel one of them. Why not he thought.

They walked off the hill and into Gareth's back yard. Gareth and Roger lived next door to each other. they had built a shed in the middle of their property line and over the years had made apple and pear wine which was given away and drunk with friends and neighbours around the firepit.

'How much wine do guys make each year'

'Well last year about 670 bottles'

Both Gareth and Roger had been down south most of the winter and spring and were amazed when they got back to see how much progress had been made on the vineyard.

'An initiative by the mayor' said Kev as he smiled at Tom.

The mayor was lapping it up. Going forward he said these are the enterprises I want to create in Mere Folly

Great said Roger if not somewhat bemused. Is this our ignorant arrogant mayor speaking or has he seen religion he thought to himself?

'You guys are great said the mayor.'

It was one of those warm summer evenings and after a few glasses of wine, Bert was enjoying himself

'You know Mr. Mayor you need people like us around you. Let's face it we are business people. The people on council and those that work for you have never been out in the real world. Its like you, a school teacher, you go to school, go to University and go and work back in school with kids, then you retire and go on council or write articles in the local paper, you don't know what it is to work in the real world.'

All of a sudden, the mayor was rather taken aback, but before he could get too upset,

'What we came here for gentlemen was to ask a favour' said Tom, changing the subject. He wanted to get the discussion round to the wine making, but more importantly he didn't want anything said in front of Gareth and Roger that could be passed on. This especially with the freely flowing apple and pear wine.

'So, what's the favour' said Gareth, 'a case or two of wine.'

'No, no, no, nice idea but no.'

'You see that vineyard over there, its going to produce a bountiful crop of grapes. We would like to plant an idea in your heads. How would you like to partner with us and make the wine?'

Again, forcing through the theory that they couldn't be all things to all people and run and manage businesses where they were a bit sketchy on the product. They were good at managing, had a little knowledge on lots of things but figured that they were better hiring the expertise needed

'You what,' said Gareth.

'Well, it would be a great project for you both. 'Expand your hobby,' added Tom, 'and at the same time, actually get paid for making wine'

'Its great making a batch of apple and pear wine once a year but operating a vineyard.'

All of a sudden Roger was thinking that this could be more like hard work.

'Heh you are making 670 bottles a year already, now you will have the chance make real wine, you will be true vintners' said Bert.

'What are we going to do with it' said Roger, 'we either drink or give ours away.'

'This will be a proper vineyard; we are going to sell it.'

'Who to'

'The people that come here, attracted by the vineyard by the stores by the restaurant.'

'Stores, restaurants, you've had too much wine, who's going to put that together.'

'We are' said Bert, 'with the Mayor's help, right Mr. Mayor.'

The Mayor gulped, 'Ehm, indeed.'

'You guys are nuts' said Roger 'you are not having any of my taxes.'

'What are you babbling on a about now Roger, calm down,' Gareth had seen the light. Gareth reminded him that they were going to get a piece of the action as wine makers.

'Let's face it there will only be a limited amount of wine produced by the vineyard you will have to supplement it with pear and apple,' said Jim

'What about taxes' said Roger,

'What's the matter Roger you are like a parrot, has the tax man been chasing you.' Tom asked. 'It's a good question. However, we'll get around that even if we have to give each bottle away with a $25 bar of chocolate'

'Obviously you are joking' Gareth laughed

The boys didn't'.

'What about parking, all this will go down like a lead balloon in the neighborhood. Can you imagine the people round here, they will really get bitter and twisted. They get upset when people park to get their mail. You've got no chance.' Said Roger.

'People won't need to park,' said Kev.

'That's great I can see people walking miles from the south side to see a bloody vineyard,' said Roger

'No' said Kev 'we have land for parking lots people will be bused in'

'We think the neighbour hood will drink it up' said Bert

'Hold on' said Roger, 'I thought that this was a City project.'

'It is' said Kev, thinking to himself. It suddenly dawned on him where he was going with this.

'Well how does a partnership with City work. I can imagine the City hiring us as consultants but a partnership. I am sure that will go down well with the general populace.'

'You'd better explain this Mr. Mayor' said Kev, 'as he chickened out and neatly dropped out of the firing line'

'Thanks a lot Kev' said the Mayor trying to buy time as it took him and for that matter everybody by surprise. The look on his face showed it.

'Look Mr. Mayor,' said Tom, we don't know yet whether we trust you, Roger is the same. Think about it, what would you do in our position.'

'We don't mean a literal legal partnership. What we meant by partnership Roger is that we would love you to be part of our team to consult on the vineyard as we push on with this project,'

Roger and Gareth walked back to their gardens happy to discuss their new roll as proper vintners

As the other five of them stood on the street and stared at the vineyard in the dusk, although pretty merry Jim looked across the road and said to the mayor, 'it will be good to get the road done, then we can get on with building the luxury condo.'

Though inebriated, the mayor was hoping he mis heard, 'What!' Just then his taxi rolled up.

'Thanks for the drinks' yelled the Mayor as he staggered to the taxi, the wine took over his emotions, he put his arms over the shoulders of Tom and Bert, "I have the threat of what you may reveal hanging over my head, perhaps I should just give up and be resigned to my fate.'

'You could do that but you will lose your job and status. You will have no marriage and the expense that goes with it. Will you get re elected? I doubt it,' Tom stressed. 'On the other hand, you can be involved in all our ideas and projects, which means we can build this city together, we will look after you.'

'How can I trust you guys.'

'You can't, but then again you have no option.'

The boys had a brief impromptu meeting. They realised that they had learnt a very valuable lesson. Going forward they must be very careful with phone calls and e mails but more importantly when with other people and even by themselves especially in Chat.

'We scraped through tonight, added Bert, 'hopefully when Roger and Gareth are sober in the morning they won't remember the true context, they don't want the story of their fire permit and how it was granted blabbed around, do they?

Later the next morning, Bert saw the e mail from the mayor go through to the project manager.

'For the moment it looks like the mayor is playing ball' said Kev 'mind you I don't trust the slimy bastard one bit.'

The project manager was delighted to get confirmation in writing from the mayor, the boys had come through with their promise. He was mystified at the power that these four seniors had, but for the time being he was quite content to sit back and go along for the ride. This suited him just fine and for the first time since he had worked for the city he had a comfort zone in that he was being allowed to do his job without being managed to death. He called the boys in to finalise the details of the vineyard project.

The next day, at a special meeting of the special projects committee the mayor explained the Vineyard project

'A couple of quick questions' said councillor Green.

'Firstly, where's the money coming from? and secondly, what happens when people question where the money is coming from.'

'Where do we usually get the money from' snarled the mayor 'We have just received an instalment from Inc. They have to pay up or else we will make sure that they never own or build anything here again'

Rather coyly and obediently, the councillor responded, 'I just wanted to make sure that there was enough there of course'.

7.

One thing about Chat was that the large windows provided a beautiful view of the parking lot.

'I see that we are having some repairs to our road' Kev said as they sat in their usual spot in Chat looking through the window.

'The city only dug the bloody road up last year' said Bert.

'I know that but according to a note I got through the door the initial course they laid failed so they have to re do it.'

'Whose fault was that.'

'Obviously, the contractors.'

'How do you know that,' said Jim

'Well, it stands to reason, doesn't it' argued Bert, 'they were supposed to do the repairs two months ago but nothing happened. Then we get another note with revised dates, however these dates again were missed but two weeks after that date they are supposed to start next week.'

What really pissed the guys off was that they were given revised dates again and told in no uncertain terms that they would not be able to use their drives and would have to find alternative places to park. On the given dates everybody was ready to park elsewhere. However, nothing happened, no contractors, no equipment and no communication

The good news; work eventually started on phase one around the corner, two weeks late but it started. The neighbours watched and spoke to each other going through the hassle of finding somewhere to park while the contractors dug up their street yet again.

With the street dug up to a depth of 9 to 12 inches work suddenly stopped, the days turned into weeks and still nothing was happening

E mails and phone calls peppered the City
A city employee responded, apologizing profusely. The complainants were told that the hold-up was due

to the contractor not being able to get aggregate. The response, almost to a tee, was that that wasn't the neighbourhood's fault the contractor should have had that organised before he started.

'I don't believe it' yelled one guy down the phone, 'I can't believe that you would use the same contractor who screwed up last year'

That of course went straight over her head but she did assure him that the City was on it and work would start again in a couple of days

Well those couple of days and a few more went by, the residents were getting madder by the day. More calls to the City, more apologies but as usual no communication

A day later a note was stuffed in the residents' mailboxes, again apologizing profusely but no information just a comment to go to a website for updates. The website explained the existing mess would be patched up and the project postponed until next year

The bodged-up construction project was a topic of conversation for many weeks at Chat.

On Friday, the project manager joined them. He laughed as he brought up the fact that the contractor was buddy of the mayor.

'Obviously, that's no surprise,' said Tom.

As they said, the more the contractor strung out the job the more they made.

'Let's face it,' said Tom, 'any business putting together a business plan and budget would want the contractors putting in tenders to provide bid, labour and materials and performance bonds. I bet the clowns at the city didn't insist on any and the company that screwed up was the one paying back handers to our mayor'

'Waste of time having a bid bond when they don't offer the contract out to bids' said Kev

'Not that we know too much about insurance, said Tom, 'but surely if there was a labour and material bond then the contractor would have had to make up for the lack of aggregate not the City'

'What about a performance bond,' said Bert, 'the city would have been recompensed for the lack of performance'

The boys understood why the project manager was frustrated as he told them that no insurance or surety was put in place. If it was, there would have to be a contractor selection process and due diligence carried out.

'Need I say any more. The mayor vetoed it to start with so it has just gone away as have most due diligence and credibility checks. It was not a question of whether surety was required, it was a question of whether the contractor could obtain surety.'

'Isn't there a set of insurance requirements in the contract' asked Tom.

'What contract' said the project manager, 'Now you are being silly, the mayor has built his own system coupled with his crooked councillors.'

'I don't get it' said Kev, 'hasn't anybody tried to halt or do anything about the corruption. Yes, but look how many city managers and staff have left or been fired of recent times'

Jim puffed out his cheeks, 'Amazing,'

The Boys agreed that they had to use the situation to feather their nest and make changes, controversial or not who cared.

'Count me in' said the project manager, feeling very confident. All of a sudden, he was on the right team for once, besides that what had he got to lose

'While we have you here what's the scoop on the traffic island to nowhere and where the money came from.'

'That's funny said the project manager, that's another gem. The contractor wanted some keep quiet money so they devised a plan to build something so that the contractor, the mayor and the councillors could make some money under the table. The best they could come up with was a useless traffic island and a road to nowhere.'

'Here's another thought' mused Jim. 'With contractors and machinery constructing the road why not use them to develop the vineyard site.'

'Great idea, with your influence over the mayor and his relationship with the contractor that will be a no brainer' said the project manager, tongue in cheek.'

The vineyard was owned by a company owned by the boys, they knew how valuable the project manager was to them and how valuable he would be going forward. He was offered a 10% share for services rendered and future services, which he took with pleasure. Another cog in the boy's wheel.

They had the vineyard but they could see the big picture, not only a vineyard but a country shop, a coffee shop, restaurant right next to the vineyard. They knew what they wanted and were going to do it but where would they put these structures.

'Easy' said Jim, who lived next door to the vineyard. 'Why not convert my house or even knock it down.'

'Oh great" said Bert 'where are you going to live, in a tent among the vines, herself will really be thrilled at that one.'

'Well we have been looking for a condo for some time.

'Condo' said Tom. 'That's it.'

I mean, Jim you are in Phoenix half the year, Bert you are in Hawaii most of the winter and Kev you are always somewhere else, condos are the answer for all of us'

'Perfect we can knock down my house, Bert's house, purchase Percy's house next door to Bert's which is about to come on the market and build a condo with the top floor devoted to luxury penthouses for each of us. Think of the view over the river valley.'

'You guys aren't as daft as you look' joked the project manager. Well, the boys thought he was joking.

'Leading question' said Kev, 'money.'

'As Jim said just now, easy,' said the project manager chipping in and fired with his 10% of enthusiasm.

'You own the vineyard company; you want to build the condo. The city donates the land to add some legitimacy to the projects and to make sure they can proceed. The cost of construction, material and soft costs will be provided100% by our friendly contractor who in return will be recompensed by the city as payment for the work on the roads.'

'Yes, but it's going to take a long time to get the legalities done, the design not to say the build.'

'Don't worry said the project manager give me a condo and I will take care of everything for you. It's what I do for a living anyway'.

They agreed to get together the following week to see what he had put together and review the strategy for going forward.

The boys weren't entirely confident that the project manager could bring all that was required to the table. They weren't sure whether they were giving him too much, but as they agreed, without him the project wouldn't happen anyway.

Tom was excited. 'From this we have a company that will own a vineyard, shop, coffee shop, restaurant and a luxury condo for each of us plus of course the profit from selling on the remaining condos.'

They hung on to their philosophy of a little bit of something being far better than a hundred percent of nothing.

A week later, true to his word the project manager was there. He had done a masterful job, the only thing missing was the condo design. Well sort of, he had a rendering which he didn't like. They were promised a re- vamp within a few days. However, the plan, specs, budget were all there. All that had to be added was the design and the costing adjustments

They liked the conceptual design of the condo. All the penthouses were exactly the same with the opportunity to make cosmetic changes. We need a real architect to fine tune

'Who has which condo,' said Jim

'Haven't a clue,' said Bert

'That's up to the women isn't it, isn't it?'

Reality was creeping in.

'What about the women?'

Shit, we had better tell them what's going on, hadn't we?'

The four of them had kind of discussed the idea with their wives, but just as the women had sniggered at the boys when they 'persuaded' the mayor to go along with the vineyard, they passed it off as the boys fantasizing yet again. Not that the ladies would be vehemently against it. No, they had all talked between themselves about moving, the houses were getting too big for them

The beer helped as usual on Friday in Chat as they pre planned the conversation they were going to have round the dinner table

Saturday night, eight people sat round the dinner table at Tom's. The boys figured that they had better update the wives on what was happening. Sure, they had passed on bits, but of course the ladies never took then seriously. They were even more astonished when they disclosed how advanced they were.

'You've got to be kidding so where do you turkeys think we are going to live when our houses are knocked down.' Said Bert's wife

'Good question, don't panic we'll figure it out.'

'Oh no you won't, this is one thing you guys are not touching' Tom's wife yelled

When the boys suggested that the four ladies get together with the architect and designers to start planning their new homes. there was a distinct change in atmosphere. The boys then produced the latest site plan and renderings.

'So, when can we meet the architect'

'Well, we haven't really got to that stage yet'

This was a typical of the boys as they just got carried away with things, lived their own lives and forgot to or perhaps in a lot of instances planned not to communicate. With the renderings spread out and the women taking a look at the whole concept, the penny started to drop that actually this was going to happen.

All of a sudden, the wives were involved, the draw for who had which condo took place, everybody seemed happy and peace descended. For the time being anyway.

The wives weren't letting go of the fact that the condo building was to be their new home and that and the surroundings had to be picture-perfect and practical.

'So, come on you geniuses, where do we get an architect from'

'We'll figure that out and we promise that you will be involved and have the final say'

The week following, over lunch with the mayor, the boys introduced their development to him. At the end of the meal they asked him what he thought.

'It's preposterous,' he laughed, 'you will never even get that land rezoned let alone get planning permission.'

'You are right' said Tom, 'we won't you will. '

'These are for you' said Kev leaving a pile documents on the table, 'you have a week.'

They walked out leaving him with the bill as usual

8.

Most inhabitants of Mere Folly were under the impression that the downtown was being developed to revitalise the city, utilising independent specialty outlets, artisan stores, restaurants and such.

A developer from the east, with relatives in the area had noticed over a number of visits that this small place was run by what he believed was a bunch of simpletons. He saw an opportunity to invest, so over time he bought a couple of properties and some pieces of land in the downtown area with a view to taking over the whole area

Used to bribing his way to get what he wanted and after spending even more time in Mere Folly researching and watching the council in action, he saw in the mayor somebody who was ripe for corruption.

Pierre was one of those affable, gregarious, get on with anybody type guys with the gift of the gab. Plumpish, bald headed with his steel framed round glasses he was a modern version of Mr. Pickwick.

It was about a year into the mayor's reign. Pierre made the initial breakthrough by inviting him to lunch. The mayor was captivated by Pierre who painted the picture of working with the him and the city to really develop its downtown. The mayor arrived back at his office absolutely glowing, it's nice to be recognised by people who understand business.

Pierre had done a masterful job.

When he arrived home that evening Mrs. mayor was glowing as well. She showed Mr. mayor the flowers that had just arrived, look, they are a mass of colour, who is this man, Pierre?

Mr. Mayor told her the story, 'he oozes class,' he said. Just then the phone rang, 'we would love to' Mr. Mayor said. Guess who, it was him, he said he would like to meet the lady behind the throne, we are having dinner with him later.

'Oh, what a charming man' she said as they got in the car, it's about time we mixed with more people apropos our social standing.

Whenever he was in town Mrs. Mayor was taken to dinner and the gifts grew from flowers, to weekend trips to the odd holiday in five-star hotels in glamorous resorts in keeping with, as she insisted Mrs. Mayor's social standing

The day eventually came when Pierre brought up the question of his dream of developing the whole of the downtown. He introduced the mayor to the development company Inc. that was going to control the whole enchilada. As Pierre well knew, the mayor had no background in any of this and really hadn't a clue what was really happening.

A parcel containing cash would be delivered to the mayor just prior to a council, planning or zoning meeting. Gradually other councillors were brought into the mix. Once they saw a box of cash in front of them, due process followed and the approval whatever it was for went through

Inc. had had its own different ideas, Inc. wanted office buildings with lower building costs, more guaranteed income with less risk.
The members of the committee were not exactly elected for their brains or morality, they accepted the gratuitous honorarium willingly.

The mayor and his councillor friend sent each other e mails from time to time congratulating themselves on how they had controlled the council, the smart bits that the council didn't know about and photos of the odd box of cash. Seeing a photo of an open box with cash in it caused the boys to take a look at the mayor's mail box. Of course, he was too dumb to clear this sort of stuff from his phone.

'So that's how and why the downtown became what it is and where the funds came from.' Said a fuming Bert.

That's the vines planted said Tom as the boys surveyed the Cote de Mere Folly. What a beautiful sight, a hill with all those vines in the middle of a city overlooking the river.

The mayor was there as well. 'You know you guys were right, I am glad you talked me into this. There have been lots of people wandering by taking a look at what's going on. I'm glad I worked with you on this'

Bert was not exactly happy with the Mayor. 'You had no bloody option, but the bonus for you is that we are letting you get he kudos for this little enterprise.'

The mayor smiled, he didn't care what those cretins thought, sooner rather than later he would be rid of them and really take control, until then he would suck up to them. Deep down though he really was pleased that the vineyard had been set up, Although Mr. and Mrs. Mayor hadn't a clue about wine they did realise that it had a certain aura about it, so they were often seen there posing amongst the wine connoisseur wannabees.

'There is no way I'll ever trust that bastard.' Bert muttered to Tom.

'Remember that.' Tom whispered back

They were in Chat; Jim was right in it doing his usual suggestive chatting up routine to the waitresses. Whether they were actually embarrassed or just treated him with the contempt he deserved was difficult to gauge as they didn't want to ruin their chance of a tip. The other boys as always were embarrassed, they joked that one day he would go too far and end up in jail. When Jim was in this zone the boys gave up talking to him as he never listened to the general conversation, his mind and eyes were elsewhere when a woman walked by. They also knew, not that it would ever happen, that if one of the waitresses took him up on his offer, they would be having a whip round for a coffin. Fortunately, for all concerned, the waitresses new him by now, figured he was harmless, turned and went back to their duties.

The conversation turned to the Mayor's vision of the downtown.

'I am sure that the initial plan for the redevelopment of the downtown area called for cutesy retail stores, galleries, restaurants and such like. A far different cry to what we have now.'

'What happened?' said Bert. 'what went wrong?'

'Well,' said the mayor, lying through his teeth, 'the city needed the money so it let a developer develop and we ended up with what we have now.'

'But it's a bloody business park full of office buildings said Bert, not what was envisioned or wanted by the citizens of Mere Folly

'Didn't Pete Earlsdon buy a building there for his clothing store.'

'That's right he did.'

'What happened to him' Jim asked the mayor.

'Oh him, we had some right battles. In the end he moved on.'

'Come on you turkey tell everyone the truth. What really happened was that you and the developer wanted his building for a high-end doctor's office so you taxed him to death and put onerous by law requirements on him'

'He deserved it said the mayor. We gave him a good offer.'

'Bullshit' said Tom 'you kept threatening him and bullying him wanting more of his profit until he couldn't stand it anymore moved to the west end.'

'Now look at him three years later his business is booming'

Bert lost it with the Mayor. 'You are an idiot, that's why we despise you. What did you get out of that deal?'

Obviously, they knew, but didn't want the mayor to know that.

'We should really turn up the heat, you should be in jail.'

For once the mayor didn't say a word and looked contrite and humble.

It was a Mexican stand-off of sorts; the boys didn't want the Mayor to remember or understand that his phone was being monitored and the Mayor couldn't do or say anything as he didn't want to chance that the boys would start disclosing what they knew.

To the boys it was obvious that the Mayor was steaming inside, however he knew that he couldn't do or say anything.

However, they still asked the leading question as a test to see how loyal the mayor really was

Bert was still after the Mayor. 'Come on Mr. Mayor explain to us how the developer got the job. What gets to us is that the downtown area is just a business centre. In essence the only people going downtown now are those going to their lawyer, dentist, doctor or insurance broker. These people don't spend money in the area except for parking, they are in and out. How can we drive out the office tenants and attract visitors, tourists and entrepreneurs just like the farmers market, we even heard a rumour that you clowns in City Hall want to move the market to some of the land the City owns on the outskirts? The downtown should be as vibrant as a summer Saturday morning all year round. It's not, the only visitors are those going for root canals – people don't care, there is nothing downtown to attract people. Lots of people go for walks, run or ride bikes by the river, passing right past the downtown'

'What river, said Tom, he was as pissed off with the Mayor as Bert. 'I bet it's not even noticed, most of the time there's hardly any water there anyway, its full of weeds and the vegetation is running rampant. In fact, you can literally walk across the river on the green stuff.'

The Mayor had had enough, as he got up to leave, he fired a shot at them telling them that they were never satisfied with what the council had done for the people of the city.

'Again, you wonder about the bastard; another slush fund built by the mayor and still he wouldn't tell us the truth said Bert, which really upset him.

'Well,' said Tom, 'there are two ways to skin a cat. Remember he still hasn't twigged that we see everything that goes through his phone.'

The boys were itching to nail him and let it out that they knew about his dealings with the developer and how he built his slush fund, but however much they wanted to, common sense prevailed and they kept their mouths shut.

'So, from now on we will utilise the councillors' slush fund.

'But I go back to Kev's question,' said Tom. 'What was that,' asked Bert.

'How can we drive out the office tenants and attract visitors, tourists and entrepreneurs just like the farmers market.'

'We do the same to the office tenants as they did to Pete, we tax them to death' jumped in Tom. 'We get the City to increase the taxes on all the downtown buildings. The developer will have to increase the rents, which will drive out the tenants, they will leave and so will the developer. We can take over the buildings and turn the downtown into a tourist destination to compliment the proposed river valley project.'

' What are tourists? Asked Jim. 'I mean what if you live locally and pop in to do your shopping, these shops won't be the type that you would want to nip around the corner to grab your daily necessities. Whether you live miles away or locally, who cares where you come from as long as they attract people and we make it easy for them to get here shop, eat and spend their money.'

Magic said Tom.

9.

The boys were out for one of their impromptu meetings with the Mayor which consisted of a walk along the river from city hall to one of the road bridges about a mile downstream

To anybody passing by it was the Mayor going for a walk with a bunch of average Joes and getting some exercise

'Look at the river, or what's left at it.' Tom was on a crusade. 'As we have said many times you can almost walk across it. It's a mess, look at it it's virtually solid vegetation, even the ducks and birds can't travel down the river. Is that what you meant when you told us the other day that we are not grateful. Grateful for what, why don't you get it cleaned up, chop down the green mass and get the river flowing again.'

The mayor's attitude had changed as he needed to suck up to the boys. 'It's alright for you guys you don't have to deal with the tree huggers. I have to think of re-election they can create a big fuss.'

'Are you nuts' said Bert, 'what about the normal people out there, most of them would love you to clean up the river and make it useful again. We are all for protecting and looking after the environment, it's the tree huggers that are the problem. Basically, they are vandals searching for an excuse to damage property, generate carnage and generate trouble using environmentalism as justification'

'With all the time they spend tied to fences or sleeping on somebody else's property, don't they have job's' added Jim

'I presume that's a rhetorical question,' said Kev

'Canals' exclaimed Tom, 'I don't know why but I was thinking of our chat the other day on the downtown area, Kev talked about dentists. I always associate with root canals.'

'Ok' said a bewildered Jim.

'Canals' called Tom, 'have any of you ever been to San Antonio in Texas. Look at the canal there. Not the weed infested bog that we have.'

'What's this got to do with dentists and root canals' said Jim still puzzled.

Have you ever been to San Antonio Mr. Mayor?

'No but I've seen pictures and read about it. I do see where you guys are coming from.

'Good' said Kev, 'just think cafes, galleries, artisan showrooms and shops along the river. There is nothing like it in this area tourists would flock here.'

'I get it now and I like it' said Jim, 'tell me more.'

'We have the base for a canal' said Kev, 'the engineer inside getting the better of him'

San Antonio has shops, cafes restaurants. Open all the time.

'We could do the same' said Bert 'with boats in the summer and ice skating in the winter. Imagine skating up and down the river just like the Rideau in Ottawa.'

The mayor even smiled, 'I think you have something here.'

Indeed, 'said Kev, 'it's a great idea but there isn't a great deal of water flow, it's not a major river and there isn't one nearby as in San Antonio. How can you make it happen?

Jim was really excited, 'why couldn't we make it happen, just think, stores, cafes, restaurants, tourists, money. It would be available year-round. Summer and winter, floodlit at night, just think the kids and their parents skating and playing on the ice.

'But our river has degenerated into a weed infested bog,'

For the umpteenth time and they kept drumming it into the Mayor.

'Whose fault is that? asked the Mayor getting even more agitated but holding it in as he needed to be considered a member of the team.

'Bloody obvious' said Bert, 'you clowns in City Hall listening to the bloody tree huggers. Who cares about the tree huggers what do they bring to the community.'

'Absolutely nothing,' said the mayor, 'in fact they cost the taxpayers money.'

'They have nothing else to do but create dissention and ruin natural habitats by trying to create them, let's face it they have never lived in the real world.' Bert was on his tirade. 'Spend money, create expense yet never bring anything to the table. Look at that so-called garden on the path way. All it is is a patch of soggy grass and bulrushes. Thousands to create, now gone derelict and rotting because the majority didn't want it or even know it was being built. Therefore, nobody cares enough to look after it.'

'You are right' said the Mayor and in a moment of emotion, 'I was looking for ways out of this mess with you reprobates but I now think that we can work together.'

Jim stuck his finger down his throat, he was convinced that the mayor was full of bullshit. 'Perfect, but remember who has the hammer,' he emphasized

'Ok' said the Mayor, 'let's do it, but the leading question is how do we do it'

The next morning the boys met the project manager for breakfast and explained the concept. They asked him if he knew an architect designer who could draw up plans for a development as large and diverse as what they were dreaming and in addition design their condo. It has to be somebody who can keep his mouth shut.

'Actually, I do know the ideal person, my cousin. The beauty of it is, my cousin is not from round here.'   'Where's he from?' asked Jim.

'Not a he, she's a she, I know for a fact that she has done projects in the States and in Europe.'

'Oh great! a relative who needs a job,' mocked Ken

'No, far from it, I don't know whether she would be free enough to fit a project like this into her schedule. She is an architect who has designed, amongst other things, sites round old derelict areas, around canals and canal basins and brought them back to life.'

'What about condo's, that's a key element in the scheme of things.'

A couple of days later the boys received e mails with pictures and details of her work. A few days after that the five of them were having one of their walks outside city hall away from the ears of all and sundry.

'Let's walk along the so-called river,' said Kev 'we need to discuss it.'

'Look at this piece of junk,' said Jim nearly walking into a large piece of rock, described by the city as art. '

'There's another waste of bloody money' said Jim 'why do we need it and what purpose does it serve.? 'What are you trying to do Mr. Mayor, appease every bloody demographic so that they will vote for you, just like the tree huggers.'

'Don't talk to me about them' said the Mayor 'they are the bane of my existence. '

'Well why don't you do something about them, bully them like you do with most people that stand in your way. Normally you don't listen to anybody, you just get on with going against the grain of what the normal citizen wants and or needs.'

'How do you propose I get rid of them,' said the Mayor, my councillors and staff spend an inordinate amount of time dealing with their stupid questions, protests, letters, complaints.'

'That's fine coming from you, I nearly feel sorry for you' said Tom, 'do what you always do just go out and nail them. I bet you will get lots of votes for that'

They walked over to Chat for a beer and discussion. As they walked in there were only two other people in the place

After exchanging the usual pleasantries with Charley, the bots ordered their beer. Kev, the engineer, then updated the Mayor on the architect that would be putting together a conceptual plan and designs.

'That will never work said the Mayor you will be fighting the tree huggers continuously. Anyway, I have to go' he said as he finished his beer,

'I'm off too' said Jim I have a tee time.

'Hold on' Mr. mirth and congeniality' said Tom, 'that's another reason why I don't trust you. Last week you were all emotional telling us that you now see the light and want to be one of us. What you think really doesn't matter anyway. One way or another, as long as we get planning permission and funding from the City and province we don't have to like you'

Then Bert chipped in, 'Jim I really don't give a shit about your tee time. You can play golf or chat up young women anytime, this is critical.'

The chink in the armor of the boys didn't register with the mayor, he was too busy thinking about his own situation and how to get in the good books of the boys.

'I know I sound like a broken record, but the problem is,' said the Mayor, 'the tree huggers whine about everything. Every time we try to do anything they bitch and moan to the media the soft centers all feel sorry for them. The politicians, especially this communist government we've got only care about getting votes at the next election. These tree huggers are very clever at protesting and getting their way, they appeal to the public and if they don't get their way threaten people in a most intimidating but indiscriminate way, sowing seeds of discomfiture and wrongdoing.'

'You know Mr. Mayor, we still think that you are a nasty piece of shit,' then Bert tempered his outburst, 'but at times I really feel very sorry for you, it's sometimes very difficult to bully and not get your own way'

Tom pushed the boat out yet again, 'How do we handle these clowns before they actually destroy the environment and culture that many people have been brainwashed into thinking that they are protecting. I mean look at the river it's a nightmare. Remember, years ago kids would skate on it, not now. Imagine, as we have said many times, Christmas time, floodlights along the river. Skaters stopping for a hot chocolate. That's our culture not a slew full of rotting vegetation and garbage.'

'Whatever you say Mr. Mayor, we are going to develop the river valley, it's decided' said Jim, 'we are going to attract business and tourists and put Mere Folly on the map. it's about time we stopped bullshitting and got moving instead of talking'

'Come on bright sparks' said the mocking Mayor regaining his confidence. 'How are you going to do it?'

'Let's get this straight you, pompous ass' said Bert, 'we are all going to do it or rather the City is going to do it. It's easy, we develop it and tell the media that it's for the benefit of the city as the present river valley is a disaster.'

'Mr. Mayor, tomorrow get your staff to do a report on all the bad things that the river is doing to the environment, culture and City in general. Then we can construct the canal as we want it under the pretense that we are doing it for the benefit of the tree huggers, a bit of grass here, a few animals and birds there they will love us'

The City fathers met and the concept was introduced. The staff did a great study that condemned the state the river was in. The

commentary in the local paper helped stir the pot, in the weeks following the letters to the editor from the tree huggers flew in. The City responded by asking the citizens if they wanted their downtown to be a desolate jungle.
The tide turned, the majority of citizens really liked the concept, the river development really appealed and the development took off.

However, behind the scenes the tree huggers were creating their usual discontent and planning vandalism. They had nothing else to do, living unhappy lives for one reason or another, jealous and upset at people who were enjoying their lives and doing anything they could to gain publicity and sympathy. They really didn't care about anybody, they rather enjoyed looking for trouble and costing the province money.

The mayor popped in to see the boys at their Friday afternoon soiree at Chat. 'Gentlemen,' he whispered, 'these idiots are getting on my nerves, phone calls, complaints, stopping me in the street, planning protests.'
'What's the matter Mr. Mayor, as we have told you before why don't you just go out and bully them like you do normal people.'

He got up, 'I've had enough of you lot, I don't care what you say or disclose I've had it.'

'Sit down and go on' said Tom standing up, putting an arm round his shoulder and easing him back into his seat. 'C'mon Mr. Mayor, there aren't too many people in here but don't get carried away and excited. If you want to live with us, remember you have no option, then you have to live with our sense of humour'

'If that's humour' said the mayor 'the'

'What were you going to say' interrupted Jim 'before we rudely interrupted you. Now carry on.'
'Alright' he said quietly. 'I have an idea. Before we start the planning, permit and funding processes we

need to stop these tree huggers from interfering otherwise it is going to take for ever.'

'Go on' said Kev

'Well,' said the Mayor, 'I was watching a movie the other night and as we were talking about the tree huggers this movie came to mind and what the theme of it was.'

'Were you watching the movie with your wife or herself? Asked Jim.

'For the second time,'

Kev had to persuade the mayor to ignore Jim who was still upset at having to miss his game of golf.

'Why don't we infiltrate the tree huggers and see if we can find out what they are up to. '

'Oh, great which one of us is going to dress up and do that' said Bert.

'Look do you want to hear me out' said the Mayor, 'getting back to his irritated state.

'Ok, ok shush guys, hear him out' said Tom.

'My nephew likes to do the odd bit of protesting against the status quo but at the moment he is a bit ticked off with two of the old women who tend to run the whole show. The other thing is he needs money as he hasn't got a job, he's a professional student'

'Mr. Mayor promise him a job somewhere with the City, he'd fit right in'

'You got it he said, no problem.

Tom shook his head, 'I was joking you pratt.'

'But I am serious, think about it. He won't last long, hates working, but it will be long enough for him to make some cash and give us we hope some useful information' 'We can circulate the rumour that the City is going to do some reclamation work to the river with a view to getting rid of the vegetation that is clogging it up.' 'We can make it easy for them' said the mayor and put a useless piece of equipment out there by the river.

'This is pure genius' said Tom, 'you are a devious bastard aren't you Mr. Mayor'

A couple of weeks later, same time same place, with the creative juices flowing the Mayor was quite cheery and excited as his ploy had been very successful and he couldn't wait to fill the boys in with what his nephew had reported back to him.

'Evidently, once the real heavy construction work started, the tree huggers were going to chain themselves to a piece of equipment.' My nephew suggested we put tarpaulins over it. He will suggest to the delinquents that they camp there. This will make them un popular not only with the City but also with the locals.'

'How do we know we can trust the prick?' said Bert.

'He may do stupid things in our eyes' said the Mayor 'but he's not that stupid, in fact I get the feeling that someone amongst the crew is getting on his nerves and he is seeking revenge'

Next day an old dozer ready for the knacker's yard was literally dropped by the river right across from City Hall at the side of the pathway by a rather expensive looking residential condo. The tree huggers thought that this was a golden opportunity, they would have shelter while they did their stuff.

Four clowns with chains and padlocks rolled up at three in the morning. Padlocked themselves to the dozer and threw the keys into the river. Sure enough their colleagues had the media there in the morning.

The sympathy was gushing out as the clowns banged their padlocks against the dozer. Of course, what they didn't realise was that all the bolts underneath the dozer were loose and rusty some in fact, were just hanging by a thread as were the tree huggers' reputations. They were feeling pretty pleased with themselves as more and more people turned up either to cheer or berate them but at least they were getting attention.

They were banging their chains and padlocks around, the clanging of metal in time with their friends who were banging drums and any bit of metal they could find to bring with them. They were quite enjoying themselves. They may have been enjoying themselves but the condo residents weren't in the same frame of mind, they were on the phone to the City, the police, the media and any body else that would listen.

One of the tree hugger matriarchs had a loud hailer and made a brief speech condemning anything, anyone, everything and everyone that she could think in the world

They bought a stove and put it close to the bulldozer to keep them warm as the chill of the evening crept in, but sitting outside is never complete without a fire so one was lit. In fact, the area around the bulldozer was quite cozy and warm. The clanging then continued into the dusk when unknown to the protesters and quite inadvertently one of the manacled mob banged his padlock at the equipment for the umpteenth time. It hit the sump bolt for the umpteenth time which by then had had enough.

Black thick oil warmed by the fire poured out of the dozer down the bank towards the river. Delusion or not a small amount of liquid appears to go a long way. There was calamity as the clowns sat there covered in oil, not being able to move and yelling and screaming having created the largest environmental disaster in Mere Folly history.

Initially, most people just thought it was the exhibitionists seeking even more attention. More protesters tried to help, they all got tangled up with the chains and the more they pulled the more it hurt the padlocked clowns. The screams were for real now. The more the chains were banged against the rusty old dozer and the more the chains were pulled the more bolts and bits fell off

The media honed in, the spectators jeered, they were having a great time as people gradually realised that the tree huggers were in trouble. More and more phones and cameras were out. Firemen eventually arrived with bolt cutters, the clowns and their "friends" were arrested and made to stand around while they were sprayed with soap and water. It was sheer agony and embarrassment for the tree huggers.

Some of the local degenerates who hadn't a clue what was right wrong or indifferent then got involved, jeering and throwing mud and bricks at the tree huggers as they were being cleaned up.

'These are the guys to go to if you ever want a disaster' said Bert as he watched from a safe distance.

What a mess.

It was hardly noticed that the oil, if not pouring was making its way down the bank over the vegetation and into the river. Normally the oil would have been thick and stodgy but the stove that the clowns had brought with them to keep themselves warm and placed under the sump improved the viscosity of the oil tremendously.

It was also surprising how much oil was in the beast; it didn't help that it had been topped up prior to delivery.

Floodlights brought in to help the fire fighters, police and other emergency services see what was going on only emphasised what the tree huggers had done. The oil slick could now be clearly seen on top of what water there was in the river. Phones were flashing as were other cameras, to capture the extent of how a City like Mere Folly was totally un prepared for an oil spill, this was a catastrophe.

The social media was already milking the scenario.

Headlines were rampant the next day. 'Tree huggers destroy river valley", 'Tree huggers turn river brown" 'Tree huggers put wild life in danger"

The mayor and the boys couldn't believe their luck. An emergency meeting of the council was called.

The mayor was briefed by the boys and really milked the opportunity to lay the base for their plans. 'We all want a healthy river a living river, with clean vital water that supports a diversity of aquatic life: microorganisms, plants, fish, beavers etc. The more diverse the ecology within the river the more resilient it can be to the inevitable inflows of pollution, be them from urban or agricultural runoff, sewage or industry.' On he went 'Instead of the so-called local tree huggers who think that they know a lot but actually know next to nothing as part of the revitalization lets get experts that specialise in river restoration, who are impartial.' Whether he actually knew or believed what he was saying really didn't concern him. This was a means to an end as he waxed lyrical. 'We will improve water quality within the new canal as part of the river system and increase aquatic life, leading to a balanced and revitalised waterway.'

Unanimously approved by council and with the wave of support from the populous, the River Parkway concept and project was launched. The money dumped into the City to help clean up the catastrophe was carefully managed by the project manager and the boys to help fund the project.

The boys sat in Chat over a bottle of wine re-living the night of the oil spill. 'Great speech to council Mr. Mayor I am sure that that will be a few more votes in the coffer' said Bert.

Under the excuse of cleaning up the "environmental catastrophe" the soft costs, damming of the river, new pumping station and excavating the pathway for the new canal have all been paid for by the Federal and Provincial Governments and Insurance.

'Mr. Mayor, it is now up to you to fund the construction and development,' said Tom.

The mayor looked stunned and asked where the money was coming from. The boys explained that the taxes on all business properties in the downtown area would be increased dramatically.

'What tax increase?' said the Mayor.

'Oh' said Tom, 'we made the decision at a meeting where you left early. In a nutshell its like this' and explained their plan to him.

The mayor couldn't believe what he was hearing. Then, when Tom explained that that would be topped up from the mayor's and councillors' slush fund plus contributions from their eastern associate's donations, he almost passed out.

'Where did you bastards get that from' he cried. His mind was a blur, what's going on? everything's out there.

The Mayor was beside himself; how did these guys know or were they guessing. All of a sudden, his backhanders from the developer would come to an end.

'You can't do that, what are the other councillors going to say,' thinking of the aggravation he would get from them as they would lose their backhanders as well.

'We are guessing that the councillors are in on your fiddle' said Tom, a guess that strengthened from lucky to accurate as the mayor looked sheepish and didn't say a word.

'Fiddle' said Bert, 'a better word for it especially if the media and police get to hear about it would be "corruption".

'But what about the developer, he will be somewhat annoyed and could start blabbing'

'Boy you have a real problem Mr. Mayor,' said Kev.

Kev and the boys smiled at each other knowing deep down that the developer should take what money he'd made and run, unless he fancied becoming a celebrity over night for all the wrong reasons. They were also certain that down the road the mayor would be contacting him to do some of the work. The boys really didn't care, as long as the work was done properly and the price was right.

The City decided to sue the tree huggers for the clean up costs, obviously knowing that they had no money, but just to stick the knife in not only in the idiots who caused the catastrophe but also the collection of activists as a whole.

That didn't matter, though, the City asked the judge for punishment due to the fact that they could go out and continue to damage property. Outside the court the left overs of society with nothing else to do walked up and down with their placards. The Judge was the wrong person to upset as many years ago one of his properties had been vandalised. He had never forgotten and always sought revenge when vandals of any sort were in his court. The defence asked for a release providing that they behaved for a year.

'I tell you what said the judge I am going to let you go on condition that you behave for nine months. The defendants smiled, but the judge carried on

'Just to make sure that you behave and as I am an old-fashioned sort of guy, we will have stocks built in front of city hall and each Saturday and Sunday each of you vandals will be placed in these stocks for 8 hours a day for nine months.

There were gasps

Not knowing when to shut up, the egotistical defence lawyer had to have one final stab at the judge, "but what if it rains or even snows".

'Then you should bring an umbrella and join them, especially now its going to be twelve months thanks to your contempt and arrogance'

There were gasps but no compromise. He got out of his seat and walked out of court smiling. 'Its about time that the few inconsiderate slobs stopped making life intolerable for the many law-abiding citizens.'

The stocks were built and the first Saturday afterwards the vandals were placed in them

Initially people walked by just to see, this changed to amusement when youngsters came by and pelted them with tomatoes. Could the next case of vandalism get the same treatment; not a lot of people were prepared to find out. Of course, the rent a protester movement were out in force but they were slated by the huge number of the public who came out to ensure that for once justice was done. The police turned a blind eye as not only the clowns in the stocks were pelted with tomatoes but also the protesters

The Judge became a local hero

In the mean-time, the project manager started the planning stage for the river project.

The boys were thrilled and so were the citizens of Mere Folly who also took to the concept and were thrilled that at last there was a city council that was prepared to take on the slobs. In addition to cleaning up the river to make it a viable pleasurable attractive positive attraction for the benefit of not only the citizens and future generations of Mere Follians but also attract tourists.

The tourists arriving hadn't escaped the notice of the guys.

'With tourists arriving, we are going to have to wine and dine them and then have shops and other attractions where they can go and spend their money.'

'Great, but where are they going to park' said Kev

'Good point,' said Tom

Next day the mayor was sat beer in hand in Chat with the guys. 'I never thought of parking'

'That's been the problem with this city council for many years, you don't think about anything,' said Tom.

'Mr. Mayor, here's another opportunity we are sticking on a plate for you.'

'What do you mean for me. Its your company that is operating the vineyard and are developing it further. Now you are consulting on the river valley, obviously you will be a major part of the design and development going forward.'

The beer was working on the mayor. For once the boys didn't say anything, they didn't have to, no sarcasm or smug remarks taking the piss out of the mayor. They knew that he fully understood who was now pulling the strings.

'The city has some dead land on the outskirts. Why don't we tarmac it and bus people in,' said Kev. 'How easy will it be to acquire the land?'

'The City already owns the land said the mayor.'

'No, you are missing the point' said Tom, we know that. We want to acquire it from the City.'

'What with' said the mayor, 'there are about six parcels, that's a fair chunk of change.'

'There is no way we want to raise money out there, too many questions, too many partners too much chance of the mayor's secrets coming out, eh Mr. Mayor.'

A derisive glance was cast the boys' way

'We could involve the mayor's girl friend.'

'What do you mean girl friend' said the Mayor.

'Well she is, isn't she' said Jim.

'She's the last person I'd want to go into business with.'

'I am sensing a bit of trouble in the corridors of power in City Hall,' said Tom

'OK enough is enough, how do we make it happen.'

'We have to start the process to acquire the land and build the parking lots, then start the process to increase the taxes on the business park'

As they all left the cafe, the mayor's phone went and he took off quickly towards his car.

Tom looked at the dummy phone, 'I guess the mayor's not giving us a ride home' as they started walking across the parking lot on their way home.

'While we are talking about downtown and the crap shoot that it is, remind me' said Bert 'to ask the Mayor what was behind the building of a traffic island right downtown with a newly created road that goes nowhere Why was all that money spent and where did it come from. Now we know, I would still like to hear his interpretation of it.'

'You can be a real nasty piece of work at times,' sniggered Tom.

10.

It was the Monday night council meeting at City Hall, normally the four of them gathered around the TV.
However, this evening Tom and Bert had been bushwhacked by Percy into attending a neighbourhood watch meeting at the city police building. They didn't want to go, but they had been promising for so long and wanted to repay Percy for getting the Mayor to the neighbourhood barbecue. It was that or watch the live coverage of the council meeting
'Now isn't this better than watching Monday night football, hockey or even attending a neighbourhood watch meeting' said Kev as he passed Jim a beer. All of a sudden, we have an excuse and ulterior motive to watch this garbage'

The cops weren't bothered either, but they hosted the event just for the sake of having a meeting to show their superiors, the bureaucrats and the general public that they were doing something to mix and mingle. It was to be a social event, a general update, show a few statistics, have a cup of coffee and a donut, then go home giving the impression that the cops were in control and showing an interest in the community

They were all asked to introduce themselves. This neighbourhood, that neighbourhood then Tom and Bert almost fell off their chairs laughing as a group of five latecomers straggled in. All were well over seventy, two had a Zimmer frame, two walking sticks, whilst the other struggled to sit in his chair. They revealed that they were the volunteers that helped the police by patrolling the streets. Bert, hand over mouth asked Tom what would happen if they came across a crime, what could they do. Phone the police; by the time the police got there it would be too late. Tom asked whether they had a contact cop that monitored them or someone that they could contact and get immediate help.

'No' said the guy with the Zimmer, 'that's a good idea we will bring it up with the city police'

'They are sat over there' said a sceptical Bert, not knowing whether to laugh or cry. Why not ask them right now, isn't that the sort of thing we are here to discuss'

The chairwoman ignored Bert's comments, immediately talking about the types of crime in the neighbourhoods. Break and enter, mischief with the big one being vandalism in the parks

Then the police revealed their latest idea to fight vandalism in the parks. A cop riding round on a glorified golf cart.

Bert couldn't resist it. 'So, this strategy is enabling you to catch the drug dealers, gangs and robbers.'

'No, the cop almost shrieked these are the cyclists with no helmets and kids who are throwing stones at beavers, it's about time we came to terms with crime here.'

'Wouldn't it make sense to give the cart to the volunteers here so that they don't have to wander round the streets with their Zimmer's. At least they could patrol some ground and have a means of escape'

'Or give them the job of patrolling the river valley,' added Tom. 'They could give friendly warnings to people not wearing helmets. Not like the cops who patrol the river valley and jump out of bushes giving tickets to young people who aren't wearing helmets. Reducing young kids to tears, the highlight of their day.
What about the vandals who are bullying young kids, wrecking playgrounds setting fire to park benches?'

Bert and Tom listened in shock as the senior cop, in all seriousness, explained that they had devised a plan to help these poor unfortunate people.

'We are going to buy these problem youths hot dogs to make them feel wanted.' The guys sat there laughing and bemused.

'So, these youngsters and members of the public who rode without a crash helmet or went slightly over the speed limit would get fined. Whereas the scum buckets who terrorised, bullied and vandalised would be given hot dogs. Makes a lot of sense. Next, you will be sending down the decrepit volunteers on their Zimmer's to sort them out'

'Now you are being stupid' the little bald-headed cop, in the corner blurted out. We are helping these older people get off their couches.'

'What happens if they get injured or even killed,'

'Good point, we are all ears' said another attendee.

Tom had had enough he waded in. 'Our gallant cops are great bullying the young kids trying to stay healthy riding their bikes or perhaps dropping a wrapper while jogging. But they are scared of the hooligans who wreck and create trouble in the local parks so they give them hot dogs. Novel policing, we have in our city'

All of a sudden there was a sense of uneasiness. In the past this has always been a coffee and donuts evening now people were questioning the police and their mentality. This wasn't supposed to happen. The little bald-headed cop's arrogance suddenly dissipated.   Silence

Then another attendee weighed in, 'Where were you the other night when I phoned to tell you that there was a car with blacked out windows parked by the park on the corner by my house. There was one guy on foot and two other cars drove up. The window of the car went down, and things were being passed between people over a five-minute period. You have been encouraging citizens to report crime and help the police so I phoned up to say that I thought there were drug deals going on. The woman on the other end was very obtuse. She asked me how I knew that they were doing drug deals. Well, they are not exchanging recipes.' I said.

'I told her that she should send somebody to investigate, the cop shop was only two minutes away. Then the phone went dead. Nobody turned up. You say you want the public's help, is that reality or just window dressing, when we try to help you don't appear bothered.'

'Wonderful city we live in,' said Bert, 'if you keep to the speed limit you will hit every set of lights on red, if you want a free hot dog go to the park and vandalise something'

Then Percy interjected. 'The police are undermanned they are doing their best. Anyway, it's getting late we can carry on this discussion next month.'

That would never happen. Everybody got up and started to leave except Tom and Bert who were still sat there flabbergasted.

That was embarrassing,' Percy said to them.

'Pardon' said Tom 'so what are these meetings for to drink coffee and eat donuts and tell everybody that there is a neighbourhood watch and it meets once a month.'

Percy walked off.

By the time Tom and Bert got to the parking lot they saw the rear end of Percy's car leaving.

'Guess we upset him and destroyed his little monthly social evening. Ah well a stroll home will do us good'

'Can we give you a ride home' said a voice from a SUV. They recognised two of the older police officers

'I guess we are going to get another lecture or they will dump us in a ditch' said Bert. 'This city is in a worse state of aggravation and corruption than we thought.'

'Fancy a beer,' Tom and Bert looked at each other a little bewildered.

'They drove to a little bar outside of the city.'

They were the only people there, which compounded their nervousness.

'It was great to hear you two speak honestly tonight we never thought we would hear locals speak up about what is happening here.'

'What do you mean?' asked Tom

'We will lay our cards on the table so that you are not intimidated and will speak openly.'

Tom and Bert looked at each other, they hadn't a clue what was going on and quite honestly after the night they'd had they didn't trust anyone especially cops.

Bert thought that it must be a cop's trick to get them drunk and reveal their inner most secrets. He was sure that this was going to be fundamental to the whole evening.

The bigger of the two chipped in, 'I will just order pop then and you two can drink beer because we reckon you will be surprised at what we are going to tell you'

'Yes, but it could still be pretence'

'OK you don't have to believe us we don't want you to say anything'

'After what we heard from you and the way you expressed yourselves tonight, we felt we could trust you.

You don't have to believe us or say anything. When we heard you two, we looked at each other and afterwards we knew we had to meet and chat, perhaps we are putting our careers on the line but we have to talk to somebody'

Tom and Bert looked at each other and thought of their comments of a few days ago "don't trust anybody".

'Right, here goes' said the bigger of the cops, my name in case you didn't remember from earlier is Dennis this is Al. We have been here about two years but been members for about 15 years each

'We still don't trust you' said Tom 'I mean how can two seniors be of any use to you. It's not as though we in positions of influence or have any authority'

'We want you to go to keep going to the meetings and question the police and if councillors are there ask them questions There are things going on in this city we want brought out into the open'

'Why don't you go to your superiors with your suspicions.'

'Good question'

'We don't know how far up the tree this conspiracy goes'

'Conspiracy, now you are getting all comic strip, next you'll be bringing the twerp in Ottawa in.'

'Exactly, you are laughing at us, so will our superiors, we are not surprised. 'Let's go, I told you Jim even these guys won't listen'

'Look, let Tom and myself give this some thought, what's the best way to get hold of you. We are still trying to figure out why you are picking on us and even if we were the equivalent of the Lone Ranger and Tonto we still don't see what we can we do.'

'OK' said Al, 'we will leave you with this thought; we can't say too much publicly but we can feed you with information and you can use what we tell you any way you want. You don't have to use any of the info if you don't want to. We can meet here when necessary. Set up a what's app joint account all we will do is text the account with the day and time of the meeting '

'All you have to do is reply yes or no. If no we will understand and send another day and time'

'Sounds good.'

They worked on the What's App account. Two minutes later it was all done and ready to roll. Text book.

Next day in Chat, Tom and Bert were telling their story of the previous night's events.

'Its bullshit' said Jim, 'you don't think that the cops are on to our relationship with the mayor do you, or has the mayor gone to the cops.'

'It's too much of a coincidence,' said Kev. 'The cops didn't know that you two would be at that meeting. If they did they didn't know that you would be so vocal and they didn't know that that would lead to an opportunity to talk to you.'

'You know' said Bert 'they didn't ask us about our thoughts, they were more concerned about theirs.

Unless they are very skilled operatives, they don't appear to be concerned about us.

'You are right, interjected Tom getting rather excited, 'they see something wrong with their situation and need to vent or take it further.'

'That's right, it's the age-old scenario, seniors make good sounding boards, they can't do a lot of damage. Listen, we will go and meet them again hear what they have to say but say nothing about ourselves.'

'Remember' said Kev, 'tee total because we all tend to say a bit more than we should do after the odd pint or glass of wine.'

11.

After the euphoria of the river valley episode, the mayor was quickly brought down to earth.

The boys were enjoying their Friday afternoon in Chat when the mayor wandered in grabbed a chair and sat with them. He looked around at the sparsely filled café.

'We are up against it now,' he said quietly

'And why should that be' said a relaxed Tom.

'I have just had a phone call from the downtown developer, he's just heard about the proposed tax increase'

'Amazing how these rumours start,' said Bert, 'obviously security and privacy aren't that strong in City Hall. Why don't you conduct an investigation into the leak? It's amazing that this information can get out but you can keep your escapades with what's her name Moron quiet.'

'Makes you think,' said Kev

'You lot are sick,' said the irritated mayor.

'Listen' said Tom, 'we are more concerned about you keeping your mouth shut and disclosing snippets of information that could hurt our projects. Perhaps we should start the odd rumour about you and the Moron'.

'You really are sick. '

'We probably are. so, keep your mouth shut.

Remember there are a few insiders in City Hall who hate your guts and we could love to have a word with' said Kev lying through his teeth

The Mayor was still anxious both about the developer and the boys lack of concern. 'If this developer starts blabbing then we are all going to be in trouble.'

'No, you are the one that has acted illegally' said Tom, you are the one that has to figure out how to fight back against this crook.'

They told him that they would be pleased to help him however, it was up to him to work with them.

'Your problem is that you have done something should we say a trifle underhanded, he knows that and is threatening you. instead of standing up to him you are backing down which gives him the power to intimidate you and control you,' said Tom

'You can't let him do that, so how do you fight back, think about it.'

They kept drumming it into the Mayor, 'he says that it will put him out of business. Well, it should do.'

'He doesn't care about this city. He doesn't live here,'

'Where does he live' asked Bert, knowing full well the answer.

'Out east.'

'That says it all,' said Bert.

Out of the blue, Tom asked the Mayor, 'Who do you know at the local newspaper'.

'What do you mean?' asked the mayor.

'Let's put our heads down and do an anonymous critical letter about this guy, about what he does, that he doesn't live here and is milking the citizens of Mere Folly'

'Get to work on Google Ken', plug his name in. 'How do you spell it' said Ken.

'Here' said the mayor, as he pulled out a business card from his wallet.

'Nothing, nothing, look at this' said Ken getting excited. 'He's not exactly squeaky clean in the eastern backwaters is he. No wonder he has been dabbling his toes in small town Alberta. Let me read that' said the mayor.

'Wow' he said, 'he's certainly got a few law suits going on against him hasn't he'

'Hold on a minute. All this stuff is readily available and you idiots at city hall didn't pick up on it. Didn't you do any due diligence.'

'It never came up,' said the mayor.

'Wonderful' said Kev

Deep in thought Kev suddenly awoke, 'before we go to the media, why don't you have a go at your friendly developer.'

'I did' said the mayor,' I thought that we were friends, but then he threatened to reveal everything he knew.'

'You know you really are dozy idiot'

'That doesn't sound like our city hall bully, how easy it is to intimidate him.'

Silence.

Tom laid into the mayor, 'Bullies are great until intimidated, they have no balls. I worked with a guy like that, he was introverted, no people skills. He couldn't get his staff to work with him as they had no respect for him so he resorted to bullying. It strikes me that they are jealous of the successful people around them and as they haven't the ability to work with or compete, they resort to bullying.'

'Sound familiar Mr. Mayor.'

'You don't care what happens to me do you?' said the Mayor.

'Of course, we don't' said Bert, 'it's funny how as soon as somebody stands up to you i.e. the developer, us, you cower away. Now phone him up and tell him that he's going to be taxed properly like everybody else. If he doesn't like that and wants to sell his holdings here, we'll be pleased to make him an offer. Then you tell him that that money will come in useful to pay his legal costs as he defends his many suits out east.'

'What if he says he will disclose about the kick backs. Tell him to go ahead but he's going to be incriminated big time and that's going to cost him big time. You are giving him a way out. By the way how were the kick-backs paid to you guys?'

'In cash' said the mayor unfalteringly, as if there was an alternative. The developer dictated, it would never have occurred to the mayor to request cash anyway and the reason why. He was so dumb he would probably have taken a cheque if offered

'See,' said Bert 'I knew it, you are not as stupid as you appear. So, he's got no paper on you, so use the one quality that you are good at'

'What's that?' asked the mayor

'Well bullying of course. Get on the telephone, bully him and get him off your back.'

The charade was working, a sense of relief and bravado swept across the mayor's demeanour.

They asked Charley, if the mayor could use his office to make a phone call.

'No, I'll do it later said the Mayor'.

'No, no', said Tom, 'you'll do it now'.

Tom had been scribbling on a paper napkin; 'here you are here's a list of the points that we discussed'

'Tell him:

1. that he's going to be taxed properly,

2. if he wants to sell his holdings here you'll be pleased to make him an offer,

3. that money will come in useful to pay his legal costs out east,

4. you are going to give him an opportunity to get out of this with some money and not go to jail.'

About twenty seconds later the mayor walked out of Charley's office.

'That was quick' said Bert,

'There was no answer,' said the Mayor.

'You chickened out' said Jim,

The mayor's phone rang.

'Hello, how are you Pierre', the mayor got up to go to Charley's office for some privacy. "Hold on Pierre" off he went.

'We should have made him stay here'

'No' said Tom, 'better he has some privacy, then we don't intimidate him'

'He won't fight this guy' said Bert 'we need to know what the heck he is saying to his friend Pierre get out the phone Kev.'

As Kev brought out the dummy phone, Bert was all over the Mayor again. 'He has no option, if he doesn't confront him he is dead in the water.'

Kev listened in as the seconds, then minutes passed by.

'This is quite the discussion,' said Jim not able to hear what was being said.

'He's probably cut the guy off and is biding his time thinking of what to say to us' said Bert

'No far from it' said Kev, 'I haven't heard tabernac said for ages'

Suddenly the door opened and out he came.

'Well?'

'I really don't know,' said the Mayor.

'Didn't you tell him?' said Jim.

'Of course I did,' said the Mayor. 'I told him what he had heard about the tax increase was correct.

'He just said "tabernac", they will have to pay won't they.'

'At first, I was concerned when he said they will have to pay. I asked him who will have to pay'

'The tenants. He said he didn't give a shit, they all have long term leases'

'My initial thought was to ask what if they don't but why put ideas in his head and draw him out so I left him to it and got out while I was ahead.'

'Good man' said Tom, 'leave him to it. Whether he has the same attitude when his tenants start leaving, we will have to wait and see. Anyway, that's not our problem.'

12.

It was Friday afternoon yet again; Jim had been in a local box store earlier and bumped into a guy he used to play golf with him but hadn't seen for years. They stood there chatting, had nothing else to do so they went for a coffee.

Jim carried on relating his story, 'He worked for the local the newspaper'

'Oh great, so he was one of the comatose so-called reporters they have there' interrupted Kev,

'No, he was the kind of admin, bean counter there,' carried on Jim 'he was the guy that lots of companies have. The person behind the scenes who sees what's going on, filled in the blanks and knew how most of the processes worked and put his finger in the dyke when needed.'

'So, what exactly did you and your newly minted friend chat about.'

'Quite a lot, he needed somebody to talk to and I just happened to be in the right place at the right or wrong time depending on your perspective. Evidently, they treated him like dirt, didn't pay him that much but promised him plenty. Except that when he reached 65 there was no promised pension, they just punted him.'

There was not much substance to the local paper. In essence there was the odd article, the odd letter to the editor in a sea of adverts.

Jim digressed, telling the boys that one of the vandals put in the stocks actually worked at the newspaper and is responsible for editorials and placing articles. Now you understand why some of the stuff in the paper is a bit out there.

'Henry told me in a piece of so-called journalism spurred on by a couple tree huggers the paper was questioning the number of building projects going on in the city. The tree huggers' sole interest in life was to criticize anything positive happening, especially if it affected the view of a tree or piece of grass in the city.

'I've got no issues with true environmentalists' said Tom, 'we all realise that protection of the environment, trees, nature etc. going forward is critical. However, the environment is just a pretext for these people to make them appear legitimate to the gullible. They attempt to gain the sympathy of those trusting enough to believe in them. From what Jim is saying, they are in fact the largest contributor to back door information for the "journalists" and letters to the editor. Let's face it, most of the stuff in the paper is garbage, yet we should be careful just in case by accident it comes across something that we are starting to get involved in. We don't need complacency just when we are on the cusp.'

'For a start, goes anybody know who owns the newspaper.' asked Kev. 'It must be quite comfortable financially, with all the advertising income it gets, conversely it has no quality staff to spend its money on.'

'I'll ask Henry' volunteered Jim

'Great Jim, but can we find out anything on its financial state.' Asked Bert

'Hmmmmm,' muttered Jim, 'I'll see what I can do'

It wasn't too long before the boys were sat round the fire with Henry discussing the rag over a beer or two.

'The newspaper is owned by a guy who literally takes any money out and milks it for all its worth' added Henry. 'He inherited the newspaper from his father some thirty years ago and lives the good life. He has a home in the Caribbean, likes his cars and luxuries and spends, spends, spends'

'Why didn't you get out of there, you could have got a good job elsewhere?'

Henry was your typical laid-back kind of guy. If you looked in the dictionary for a description of an accountant, there would be Henry's photograph.

'I don't know, time goes by and eventually you grit your teeth and think that shortly I would be out with a comfortable pension.'

'They must have had a bunch of money coming in from all that advertising. I mean they couldn't have been paying much out for journalists.'

'Of course not, they had students and a couple of guys who did bits part time. I mean take a look at the guy who did sport. He didn't know the difference between a baseball and a football. You could tell by the way he got all the terminology and idioms mixed up especially when he used the verbiage used in baseball and hockey when writing about soccer and rugby.'

'What happened to the money, he must be pretty wealthy.' Asked Tom

'No, he hasn't got two dimes to rub together.'

'I thought you said that he had a place in the Caribbean.'

'Well he has but he spends so much money partying and entertaining over there that he had to remortgage his big place here'

'The drugs and booze flow, I had people phoning me in the office threatening to take me apart if I didn't come up with money'

'After all that you still thought you were getting a pension,' said Kev.

'But Kev there was a ton of money going through the books.'

'Don't know about you guys' said Tom, 'I sense an opportunity. Don't know what or how but I sense something.'

'Don't be silly, none of us know anything about newspapers.'

'Obviously nor does the present owner' said Bert

'We should meet this guy.'

'I wouldn't want to be there,' said Henry.

'No, we will take care of that,' said Kev

Getting hold of the owner wasn't easy, he didn't return phone calls and ignored voicemails.

'Perhaps he is too important to attend a business meeting with a bunch of locals.'

That was until Tom mentioned in a voicemail the fact that they would like to discuss his captive in the Caribbean.

The four of them turned up for the meeting.

'I thought I was just meeting you' said Dominic, as he liked to be called.

Its rather funny, sometimes you meet a person for the very first time and that coupled with what Tom had heard about him, it was instant dislike

'I was lying,' said Tom. 'Straight to the point, we want to acquire the newspaper, these are my partners' said Kev.

'Piss off' said Dominic 'you couldn't afford it.'

'Probably not, but times are tough and friends are few,' said Jim.

'What's that supposed to mean you dipstick'.

Without taking the bait, Tom laid it out. 'What if we write a letter to the editor disclosing your phony investments, unlicensed insurance, drug deals we could go on.'

Henry had briefed them well

'Get out of here, you old bastards are senile'

'No, I don't think so, we may be old bastards, but certainly not senile,' said Tom.

'You mean to say that I am going to allow a pack of lies to be printed in my own newspaper. You are bloody senile,' his mouth was twitching and drying up

'Well, perhaps not, but you are misinterpreting, we really mean the letter will go to real newspapers.'

'I told you; you idiots really are senile. What are you after?'

'Your newspaper' said Tom with a subtle smile.

We will take it over and pay you 10% of the advertising revenue.

Then all the money you have in your insurance captive can be repatriated back to Canada and you won't be taxed personally you will just have to pay capital gains.

'How do you know about,'

'It's surprising how much we do know, isn't it,' interrupted Tom 'it comes with senility. 'Think about it, in that way you have a legitimate way to bring back the money, the sale of the company, you won't have the CSA chasing you and you can pay off your debts and get your creditors off your backs'.

The guys got up in unison, 'when you are ready to do the deal just change the colour of the paper's name on the front page from blue to red,' said Bert.

A week went by, over their Friday beers, the consensus was that this time they had overshot, but sure enough two weeks after the meeting Bert stood in the street looking at the paper's name in red print.

That night Henry sat with the boys in Chat.

Who in that place is worth keeping?

'Next to nobody,' said Henry.

'Well, they do have one guy who is not bad but he is a bit timid. The editor told him everything he wrote was crap but what was really happening was that when Craig put a piece together, the editor took it, amended it bending the truth and slanting it into his own views and those of those who were feeding him with backhanders.'

'Guess who the editor's biggest supplier of content and back handers was.'

'The Mayor,' said Kev.

'How did you know?' said Henry

'Lucky guess I suppose,' laughed Kev

'I just hope that slime ball doesn't get re-elected'

Henry, don't you worry about the Mayor any more. The paper will still be supporting him.

'If that's the case then I want nothing to do with you. I thought that you guys had some credibility'

'Hold on Henry' said Tom we appreciate your integrity but the Mayor's attitude has changed.'

'Bullshit' said Henry.

An hour later, the Boys had finished explaining, in vague terms, what had happened and why the Mayor was no longer the leading player that most people thought he was. Well almost, there were still many things that the Boys thought better to withhold.

Henry appeared confused, 'you mean this city is gradually being taken over by you guys.'

'Yes, the newspaper is a big coup, but don't worry Henry as long as you look after us we will look after you.'

Henry staggered to the waiting cab not quite able to figure out what was going on

Next day Tom called a meeting.

'I didn't sleep too well last night. All this stuff that is going on and now we are going to acquire a newspaper.'

'What did you come up with in the early hours,' said Bert

'Well, it dawned on me that we need a lawyer and an accountant. '

That's big money' exclaimed Jim,

'But it could cost us really big money if we don't do it right,' said Kev.

There was silence

Does anybody know anybody.

'What's up with keeping Donald, he's done ok for us so far.'

'Hold on' said Bert, 'he's done ok with the vineyard, but that's more or less like a house purchase, we are getting involved in some pretty heavy-duty stuff, we need advice from people who have been there and done it.'

'But that's going to mean lots of money,' said Jim.

'You are sounding like a broken record,' said Tom.

'Let's face it, we are on to something here, we already have a company, but going forward, that will expand, in fact, and don't laugh, it could morph into an empire or conglomerate.'

'I like it' said Jim, 'talk to me some more.'

Bert rolled his eyes.

'All I am saying is that this company, conglomerate call it what you like has to be set up properly and structured. The, sun is rising but before it gets hot this thing has to be structured. Who is going to run it, who is going to do the books, who is going to control the Mayor and make sure nothing slips through our fingers.'

A moment's silence

'How far do we want to take this thing guys? Do we come out of retirement or sit around criticizing and watching the world go by before the tape measure and then the coffin lid snap shut on us'

Two days later they were in the lawyer's office, not in their city but downtown in the big city some 15 kms away. They sat waiting in an open plan area gazing at the cityscape from the top floor of one of the tallest buildings around.

'Why are lawyers never on time' said Tom, 'I get pissed off at them, I would break my neck to get to their office on time and then eventually he or she would send for you. Note that they never come to your office, arrogant pricks. I bet we are being charged now for waiting for them.'

'If you will follow me' said one of the receptionists.

'Nice arse' said Jim as he watched her leave the board room

'They still aren't here and the meter is still running' said Kev "arseholes".

Eventually, a tall well-dressed guy with thick glasses that hid most of his face appeared. 'Good morning gentlemen, how are we,' as his teeth appeared below his glasses.

When you meet a person for the first time you never know whether they are sincere or it's just the appropriate thing to say,

'I see I'm first.'

'No' said Bert we're already here. 'Appointment was for 10, its twenty past.'

'Good morning it's been a long time Richard,' said Bert shaking his hand. 'Good timing as the meeting could have ended before it started.'

Bert had worked with this firm over many years,

'Good job we know each other, funny, they were always on time for me' grinned Bert

'As I was saying earlier it's no good using a lawyer in Mere Folly the word and our business would be out in no time. That's why I suggested one of the largest firms in the province. Obviously, they know how to mind their own business, right' said Bert,

'Er right said Richard.

'I don't know if Bert briefed you, but we are on the cusp of taking over a City.'

'Right', smirked the lawyers, wondering if these guys were quite sane.

'We thought that we were here to put together the acquisition of a newspaper.'

'We are, but there are other situations and even opportunities that have to discuss with you. It will sound rather bizarre, however, by the time we have explained everything I am sure that even you will understand.'

The lawyers were not so sure.

Interrupting, Richard's colleague Dennis said, 'I feel I have to ask, what you are about to tell us is legal isn't it?'

'From our perspective of course it is, but we have found a few nuances along the way, so that's your job to sort that out'

After an hour and a half of the story with questions, explanations and enlightenments thrown in, Dennis just exclaimed 'WOW.'

'You are right, you are on the brink of taking over Mere Folly'

'Correct, we know that, but with your help we will do it properly. Are you up for it?'

'We are,' said Dennis, more thinking of the money rather than what was involved going forward.

'We have handled large acquisitions, sales you name it, my question is do you four, and I say this in the nicest possible way, do you know what you are getting yourselves in to and if you do can you handle it.'

'At this moment in time and that could change at any time, you are involved in literally taking over the operation of a city of thirty thousand people, a vineyard, the development of a condominium, the redevelopment of the city's downtown, a river valley and a newspaper'

The lawyers were now convinced that the place was and is being run like a joke. They didn't know whether the Mayor and his councillors were a bunch of crooks or simple incompetents. From what they were told they were both, none of them had management experience, really, they couldn't run a piss up in a brewery.

'At least you guys have run various entities, its whether you want to start working again'

'Why not, the secret is to get good people working for you just like the lady who is going to design the river valley and the condo'

'But what about the environmentalists and the council.'

'What about them, you have to realize that it's not the environmentalists it's the tree huggers, the environmentalists will be only too pleased to work with us, we will council them.

'Can you let us have a business plan on your various projects.'

'Sure, you will have it within a week.'

'What we want you to do Richard is to start work on the newspaper acquisition.'

'Ok, we will get in touch with the newspaper's lawyers and if everything goes smoothly, we should have something organized in about a month.'

'Here is a file with the pertinent information on the newspaper deal' said Kev passing it to Dennis. 'You have a week; we will be here in this boardroom same time and that is 10 am sharp to sign the initial papers.'

Dennis was about to argue, 'Just a ….'

The got up abruptly as he started to open his mouth,
'See you next week' as they headed for the elevator, the lawyers sat there shell shocked.

'That's the way to deal with those clowns, we are paying for their services, it's about time they realized that and gave us value for the money that we are going to pay them'

As they drove out of downtown, they agreed to gather the paperwork on all the projects that they had collected and meet at Kev's at two.

They went through each project one by one so that they knew exactly what they had, where they are at, who is doing what, what needs doing.

'Obviously, the newspaper acquisition is paramount we need to get it bottled up before that troll tries to wriggle his way out of it. Once we have it it becomes our means to communicate and explain indirectly what is happening.'

'Number one; running the city, the key to the door and crucial to the ability to pursue all our projects. Critical is what we do with the Mayor.'

They obviously knew he was bit of a pillock but as long as they had him by the short and curly's they had a comfort zone, 'Let's face it, he wants to maintain his status, pride and arrogance, we can help him, which will obviously help us. We should have a chat with him to tell him what we expect and see what he expects,' said Tom

Bert was concerned, 'we have to get rid of the mayor's building fiddles such as work on the roads using his buddies doing the jobs twice'

'Then, another serious issue we have,' carried on Bert, is the city sports club taking the citizens for a ride. Let's face it, the majority of sports are elitist. Many parents can't afford the cost of their kids playing at a higher level. Many go into debt to maintain the dream. Why should only those kids with parents that can afford it and buy them up the ladder have the opportunity, it's sad that some potential Gretzky's never get the chance'

Tom carried on. 'Number two; the development and operation of the vineyard. Again, we have the city to thank for "helping us" to establish this vineyard. We need to finalize a deal with Gareth and Roger to get the project going in order that we have the grapes growing on the hillside'

'How are we going to market and sell the wine' asked Jim

'Let's do it like the movie "make the wine and they will come,' said Tom

'Why not, there is another piece of land let's make it there, sell it there have a café, shop and even a high-end restaurant' added Kev

'Number three: Over the road we will be knocking down our houses to build the condo. What a view a quarter of a mile away is the river, it will be a community and a half'

'Number four: the acquisition of the newspaper'
The Mayor will be pushing planning and development permission through and the Newspaper will back it up'

'Number five: the redevelopment of the city's downtown.'

'Number six: the redevelopment of the river valley'

Just then Bert's phone rang.

It was the lawyer. 'We have a problem'

'What's the problem,' the boys' eyes immediately stared at him in unison.'

'Oh, does he, I'll get back to you.'

'What's the problem,' asked Jim,

'He wants controlling interest, 51%.'

'That's easy, tell him to piss off' said Kev, 'its 10% of the advertising revenue or nothing,'

'Well let's sit on it, what can he do if we say no.?'

'Let's get hold of the Mayor so that we can get him sorted out. We need to tell him what we want and then we can gauge his reaction and see where we stand.'

Next day, the boys plus the mayor met in the boardroom of the lawyers. They borrowed the room not only to intimidate the Mayor but also to have some privacy and make the meeting much more formal away from any prying eyes of the locals.

'How's it going?' asked the Mayor.

'Very well' said Kev, 'here is the agenda.' It consisted of the five projects and the newspaper acquisition.

'You are still going to buy the rag?' asked the Mayor.

'Definitely' said Bert.

'It will be good to get rid of that crook,' said the Mayor.

'What do you mean' said Tom, 'crook? you sound as if you know him.'

'Well he is and I do,' said the Mayor.

That's great coming from you said Tom under his breath

The boys despite working with him still really despised the Mayor

'You've opened the door' said Bert, 'so what do you know'

'All right' he said looking down at the floor.

The Mayor explained that Dominic was out with a councillor at a function. The councillor was driving, Dominic suggested that as the councillor had had a few drinks they should go the back-way home. On the way home, they were stopped by police, which was rather strange, they just happened to be around on a country road at the time the councillor's car came by. It was obvious he had been drinking, the cops breathalyzed the councillor and suggested that he shouldn't have been driving. He was scared shitless, he had visions of his career and credibility disappearing.

The councillor could see Dominic was smiling under his breath as he asked the councillor to leave it to him as he knew the cop. As the councillor sat trembling in his car Dominic wandered over to the cop, put his arm round his shoulder. Dominic suggested to the councillor, they could get out of this mess but he wanted five grand. The councillor told Dominic to tell the cop to fuck off, he would see him in court and then visit him in jail. Dominic told him that he really hadn't got any option. He told the councillor to hold on, off he went back to the police car, back he came. Dominic was full of himself as he told the councillor that the cop had told him to tell him, final offer, that he would settle for a thousand dollars cash right there and then.

The councillor was incredulous, he didn't know quite what to do. He asked Dominic who carries a thousand dollars with him and asked if he should go to the bank. Dominic asked the councillor if he had his cheque book with him, which rather surprised him. The only reason the councillor had his cheque book with him was due to the fact that the function that they had been to was a silent auction. He told the councillor to write him a cheque as he always carried a couple of five hundred-dollar bills in his wallet just in case of emergencies. He wandered off toward the car cash in hand; as he was walking back the cop car drove off,

Later, the councillor watched as Dominic looked at the photo on his phone with the picture of the cop car and the councillor's car.

'My friend Mary, the councillor,'

'You mean your fancy woman,' said Jim.

'You really are a prick,' said the Mayor.

'Well let's call a spade a shovel,' said Jim. 'The woman that you are knocking off'

'I've had enough of this' said the Mayor.

'Ok you two' said Bert. carry on, we are intrigued.

'How do you think that she got on council in the first place'

The Mayor's confidence improved as he got excited that he could actually tell them something that they didn't know coupled with a sense of relief that not only was he telling them something, but sharing something with them.

He so wanted to be friends with these characters. He knew that they didn't trust him but without realizing it he was building the relationship with the boys that he craved

'She had a relationship with Dominic. He was pretty predisposed to the odd beverage and sex. During their odd frolics in bed he would tell her all sorts of things. One of which was the story of how he had the councillor in his pocket, which led to him saying to her that she should get on council. She didn't think that she had a chance. He told her that it could be arranged. and it was

It's amazing how without any work on her part in garnering votes she ended up getting elected to council.

Let's face it the newspaper boy was a nasty piece of work as can be gauged from what he was doing to the councillor. He really was a spoilt troll and treated her like a doormat. She had literally been forced into a relationship with him. At a party one evening he preyed on her, doctored her drink and waited until she hardly knew what she was doing. He took pictures of her in various poses of undress and as was his favorite trick blackmailed her.

She had ended up having to do what he wanted but got so used to the finer things in life that his money could buy she became his mistress. In essence any of the things that he wanted done to make him money through his newspaper he would expect her to help push it through. After time she got used to it as it became a means to an end, she was enjoying the quasi glamour.

Don't forget she also worked part time at the newspaper looking after the things that he didn't want employees to see or know about.

There was one thing I recollect her telling me about was how he paid his insurance premiums and how they went to Barbados a couple of times a year to attend a meeting over dinner. Something about how he had a bunch of business owners, some very elite such as finance companies, car dealers, a chain of restaurants get together and send their insurance premiums and other money over to a company he had in Barbados. Any income he got came from Barbados not as a salary from his newspaper. I really don't understand it but it doesn't sound right to me.'

'Yes, but how do you know all this and why do you let the troll get away with dictating what you do on council.'

'Isn't it obvious, the mayor shouted almost embarrassingly, the troll was bribing was me, I was the councillor that was stopped, and breathalyzed'

'Bloody Nora,' said Bert.

'I was a bit afraid of her, knowing who she was shacked up with. From there, knowing about the story of the con and how the mayor was deceived, she thought that she might as well have a word and let him know that his secret was really not a secret. He was mortified. Not to worry she told him I can help you.'

'I was amazed that she knew everything as well.'

However, as he was to find out this knowledge gave her the strength to tell him the reasons why she was with the troll. How she absolutely detested him and would one day get revenge. That's now what drove her on'

The Mayor said he asked her why she stayed with him so long.

'Why do you think?' she asked him'

She told him not to think badly of her as she was really fond of him and that even though he was married she was sorry but didn't care.

To most people their skin would crawl, but the future Mayor was a simple sole and she knew how to pull his strings. He had been married many years and the last thing that crossed his mind was another woman taking an interest in him. This would actually blow his mind which in essence was what was happening

He told her that he was very fond of her, in fact he was falling for her in a big way. He was always reluctant to open up for obvious reasons. But eventually he did.

The Mayor was sure that their feelings for each other were mutual

'But how has none of this affair got out' said Kev. 'Surely the troll has found out.'

'He didn't, as far as I know. Remember, they had hated each other for years and as she told me many times that he was busy most of the time dipping his pen in the ink. That's what he's up to most of the time'

'Yeah, but what about the troll's wife and kids'
'I am sure that's over.'

They decided to solidify things by taking a trip together with the kids. Yes, all of them They bought a motor home and decided to drive across Canada. They got as far as PEI.

She couldn't stand him with his wife, so she kept on sending him messages.'

'What did she say.'

'Guess.'

'She told me that as a result of knowing him so well, words he couldn't resist like she needed him and she needed him in bed. She really wound him up, they got to Ottawa on the way back and he left them jumped on a plane back here and left her with the three kids to drive the mobile home back.'

'He really is garbage,' said Jim

'When she went with Dominic, she was naive but over the years listened a lot and learned a lot so when he got ballistic at her she told him to back off as she had had enough on him to nail him to the wall forever.'

She wasn't stupid, from that naivety had grown strength and a shrewdness born out of being bullied and tormented by a person she despised. Over the years though of suffering had developed a sense of non-trust. She didn't trust anybody; she only fed the mayor information that would deceive the mayor into believing that there really was something between them.

As she had been used so she started to use other people especially the Mayor.

Her character had hardened. The mayor of course was the next hurdle in her trip up the ladder and to her he was one of the rungs that she would need to tread on.

13.

The boys sat chatting in their usual corner of their watering hole.

'I was thinking about Percy,' said Kev.

'That's done and dusted,' said Tom. 'No think about it, the reason that the crows were still around was that nobody had explained to Percy the effect the crows had on other people and what his actions were doing to others'

'What's this' said Charley.

They explained

'You are right' said Charley 'it's no different to the lasagna, sorry Bert, but it doesn't hurt to look at situations from somebody else's perspective,' he left to take a phone call.

They had to go and see the troll at the newspaper office and get his perspective, but now they felt that they had the gun to hold to his head. Then simultaneously it dawned on them as they were thinking about what the Mayor was telling them and how the troll was bribing the Mayor. They couldn't let Dominic know that they knew anything. It was deflating, but they realized that the end justified the means

'There's nothing wrong with the troll sending money to an offshore company, that I know, lots of companies do it to avoid paying tax which is not illegal, perhaps morally wrong, but I bet you knowing the troll, there is more to it than just sending money offshore.'

'Yeah, but we can't prove anything, or pin him to the wall we have no concrete evidence, its all hearsay and guesswork,' said Jim, 'But he doesn't know that'

They figured it was worth it and a way to grab him by the balls

The boys walked into the troll's newspaper building.

'Is he in' Kev asked the receptionist,

'Who's he' she said.

'The big cheese.'

'Who are you' she said looking down here nose at Jim as he stood there in his tee shirt and outdated jeans.

Tom told her that they owned some of the place and that she actually worked for them. However, judging by her impressive people skills it might not be for very much longer.

'Now tell him we would like to see him'

'What can I do for you gentlemen?' askrd the troll.

He really did look and sound like a troll. Short with grizzled features, almost as if he smiled his face would crack. You know looking at some people you get that shiver up your spine and an immediate feeling that you don't like them and or trust them

'To quote the famous phrase, it's what we can do for you.'

His demeanor changed; he told them that he didn't have time for bullshit.

Tom brushed by him and walked into his office telling him that they didn't either.

The others followed and sat down Kev in the troll's chair.

His voice was monotone which matched his personality. 'What do you want, you arseholes, you have my conditions, if you don't like them tough. Get out or I'll get the cops and have you thrown out'

'We would simply like to discuss the purchase of the newspaper,' said Bert

'As I said before, I told you the terms.'

'We realize that, however certain information has come to our attention that will make the negotiations much easier.' said Tom

'What are you on about now,' said a bemused troll

'Your offshore dealings' said Tom. 'We just want to know that if we buy the newspaper, who do we buy it from; you, the offshore company, creditors and then what are you going to do with the money.

Keep it offshore? Let's face it if you repatriate your money and pay the tax you won't have enough to settle your debts

'How do you know about all this' said the troll.

'Lucky guess' said Tom.

'Who told you' said an angry troll his wrinkled face getting redder by the minute.

'I told you' smiled Tom, 'lucky guess'

'We will make it easy. If you sign the newspaper over to us, we will leave you with your nest egg overseas'

'You bastards.'

'No, No,' said Tom, 'think about it, if we weren't prepared to help you the newspaper would go under, you would have to "disappear" and have Revenue Canada chasing you forever. This way you can survive. Sign this letter of intent and I will get our lawyers to finalize the deal,'

They left, smiled at the receptionist and got into Bert's car.

'How did you know all this' said Kev 'why didn't you tell us.'

Tom laughed, like I said to the troll I just guessed. It didn't really come to me until he got bitter and twisted at us.

So, with a virtually bankrupt newspaper and considerable debt. Experience had taught them that the best place to start was the creditors. Two weeks later the bulk of the creditors were onside with the new owners. They could see the point. They could lose all the money owed to them or work with the boys. Staying in business would allow two things. One a chance to get all of their money back. Number two a chance to make money if the newspaper prospered

As the boys explained and illustrated there was adequate income to cover expenses and pay off the debts. The troll did plough all the income into the company, the only problem was that the company happened to be registered offshore. Not so good for the creditors as they were rarely paid, however great for him as he didn't have to pay any Canadian tax.

The four seniors had over two hundred years of high-level business experience between them. They had proved they could carry on running a business, so why waste all that pedigree. Many seniors are put on the shelf by immature, inexperienced and jealous people who want them out of their way so that they can steal their positions. Businesses should be using those people not abusing them.

There are lots of sixty, seventy and even eighty-year old's' out there still working hard and doing a great job. Look at Warren Buffet, sports teams' managers and coaches amongst many others. They hire the nerds to do the work, while the people with the experience and street smarts manage and mentor them.

14.

Bert and Tom would go and have the occasional coffee with the cops. Nothing much was said as both parties were wary about each other or that's the way it appeared to them.

During one of their Friday soirees Bert admitted that he was ready to call off the thing with the cops

Jim and Kev wondered why.

'Come on' said Bert 'we each sit there like stuffed dummies talking about the weather, politics, we might as well sit and talk with you. It appears to us that we are wary about each other, or perhaps, said Bert we are wary about them but they are making us feel that way,'

'What do you mean' asked Kev.

'It's as if they are playing a game to get us to disclose what we know by forcing us into a corner. They appear to be our friends and so they are making us feel guilty for not saying anything.'

'They are not saying anything either' said Tom, 'we know that and they know that but psychologically they can grind us until we feel so guilty that we will say something of use to them just to make them feel good. They do it all the time with crooks.'

'You should almost go pre-armed with something useful to say or some information to give them,' said Kev.

'That's a good thought, but what, any ideas' said Tom

Between them they couldn't come up with anything that could be considered remotely useful to the cops.

'That's how we are when we sit with them, we haven't a clue,' said Tom

'I don't know' said Kev, 'I still don't trust the police. On the surface they appear helpful but they are just like a secret society'

Some days later, Bert and Tom arranged to meet the cops, not in the usual coffee shop but at Chat

'You two are nuts' said 'Jim I thought that you wanted to keep your discussions quasi secret.'

They knew they did, but something was eating away at them. As they kept saying, their discussions had always been low key, they had been determined not to say anything but the cops who initially asked for their help never said too much either, it was like playing blind man's bluff. The initial plan was to go to a coffee shop and stay stone cold sober, not say too much and wait for them to open up perhaps they are thinking the same about the boys. However, they had had enough and decided to piss or get off the pot They didn't want to spend another hour, even a day let alone a week

socializing with mundane cops. They still had that gut feeling about them.

'It's the same as business,' said Bert, 'if it's too good to be true it probably is, that's why we are going to meet at Chat and as in the movies bring them out into the open.'

Bert and Tom sat at their usual table and were drinking their usual beer when the cops walked in.

'Neat place' said Al 'so you've been here before, the waitress told us you had your own table'

'We come here now and again the pizza's pretty good'

'How's things' said Dennis.

But before they could answer, Charley wandered over,

'Tom, there's a phone call for you.' Excuse me said Tom, as a shiver of concern went through him, who would know he'd even be there.
'Who is it'

'How should I know' said Charley, 'I have a hard-enough time understanding you guys let alone keeping tabs on your friends'

'Tom it's the Mayor.'

'What do you want, how did you know I was here.'

'I walked in and luckily you guys nor the cops saw me, so I got out quick'

'How do you know that they are cops'

'What are you talking to them about interrupted the Mayor'

'None of your bloody business' whispered Tom trying hard not to get excited and shout.

'One of them is the cop who stopped me and bribed me,' shouted the Mayor

'You are bloody kidding.'

'Don't say thank you for tipping you off' said the Mayor.

'Sorry' said Tom, 'I'm shell shocked and trying to thinking of what to do.'

'Easy' said the mayor, 'watch your step, I wouldn't trust the police in this city as far as I could throw them.'

'Give me a call later.'

'Ok" said Tom 'and thanks.'

The Mayor smiled to himself and drove off eager to hear why they were meeting

'I'm sorry guys' said Tom when he got back to the table, but we have to go.

'We will fill you in next time we meet'

'Is everything alright' queried Al.

'Kind of' said Tom as they left. The cops were expecting details but the boys were gone

'What's going on?' said Bert,

'You won't believe it, I'll tell when we are away from the café.'

'Are the cops still there?'

'Yeah, they'll love you though,' said Bert

'What walking out on them, that must happen a lot to them,'

'No, leaving them with the tab,' Bert laughed, 'oh they're good for it'

Bert couldn't wait to find out what was going on. As soon as they got round the corner, he asked who was on the phone

'The Mayor', said Tom.

'The Mayor, 'said Bert 'how did he know you were in Chat and why rush off'

'You didn't tell them anything did you.'

Without waiting for an answer, he started to tell Bert what the Mayor had said

'Sod off' said Bert, 'I knew it, I told you didn't I, always listen to your gut my old man used to say, you'll never go far wrong.'

'Good job I told them my lasagna story, first time I've actually seen them smile.'

'Who wouldn't' said Tom sarcastically

They agreed that they had dodged a bullet and could see Jim and Ken giving them a hard time over this.

'Phone them' said Tom, 'we'd be better having a meeting on my deck.'

'I'll phone the Mayor; we should know if there is anything else he knows.'

The boys were relatively subdued as Tom passed the beer around. 'So where do we go from here'

'Well' said Kev, 'not wishing to gloat, but this appears to have been a set-up from day one.'

'But a lot of the stuff we are doing now wasn't even a figment of our imagination when we went to the cop shop. So, what could they want us for, I don't get it' said Bert.

'That's what I can't understand' said Jim, 'Why are why the cops seemingly interested in you two. What did you do in the cop shop that night.'

'Not a lot' said Tom, 'As you know we criticized them a fair bit, but so did one or two other people, they wouldn't put a couple of their undercover snoops on us for that and besides that, surely they wouldn't have had enough time to put it together.'

'Think about it, if Percy hadn't have gone home in a huff and left us to walk home the cops wouldn't have had the opportunity to meet us.'

They were convinced that there was something more sinister happening

'Sinister' said Kev, 'you're sounding like James Bond.'

Perhaps' said Tom, 'but why. I could understand if it came from the newspaper saga and acquisition but that came later.

Just then there was a creak and up the deck stairs came the Mayor.

'Gentlemen,' said the mayor feeling supremely arrogant as he felt had a bit of a leg up on them. 'So, he said nurturing his beer bottle, how did you guys get so friendly with those undercover cops.'

Basically, all we did was go down to the neighborhood meeting at the cop shop, Percy got upset at something we said, left us to walk home and these cops came out of nowhere.

'But they are cops' said Bert.

'I suppose they are' said the Mayor 'but normal cops don't set people up to bribe them'

'Ok' said Tom 'that's too much of a coincidence. You recognizing that guy as the cop that set you up'

'I agree said the Mayor, perhaps there are coincidences but I will never forget him, I still have nightmares about that night more so than what you are doing to me.'

'Yes, but, is that cop still bribing you and got you in his pocket' asked Bert. 'Perhaps you set this thing up to get back at us.'

'Hold on', said the Mayor 'would I have warned you.'

'Could be double bluff,' interrupted Kev

'You really are getting James Bond again aren't you' said Tom

Changing the subject, Bert put it out there, wondering if they knew about the Mayor's relationship with them.

'Relationship,' that's a good word for it said Tom. This is fun

'Fun' said the Mayor, 'you have a couple of undercover operatives chasing you and it's fun'

'Yeah, but you have to understand' said Tom, 'we haven't got much time, the tape measure is ticking.'

'Let's face it if we don't go for it and have some fun, we will be sat on the sofa watching tv with the snow blowing outside asking ourselves why we didn't go for it or them' added Kev.

'If we upset somebody or bend the law what the heck. The life tape is getting shorter.'

'That's right' said Bert, 'when we first got together it was this long, now it is only this long as Bert illustrated by holding his hands apart'

'My minds still boggling' said Tom 'but let's lay it out so that we can grasp what's going on with these cops and figure out where we are going from here'. So, they bribe and have something on the Mayor. According to you Mr. Mayor they haven't tried to blackmail you, I mean a person in your position it doesn't make sense,'

'I know I'll probably regret asking this' said Tom 'but what about Percy, he got us down there and left us. Let's face it he's big with the cops, he's not keen on us because we criticize the Mayor, the Government, the cops. We even criticized banks one day and then he told us he was a retired banker'

'Do you remember when Percy told us that he had told the cops that the city manager was having an affair. I wonder if he did tell them.'

'Probably' said Kev.

'Hold on,' said the Mayor. 'How did you know the city manager was having an affair. We really didn't but I guess we do now' said Tom, 'is there something else that we should know about.'

'So that's where the leaks have been coming from, more by luck than judgement' said the Mayor, 'but that's what's been happening'

'The city manager was having an affair; he came to see me because he was being blackmailed and I am sure that you can guess by who.'

'It doesn't take a rocket scientist,' said Jim.

'The bastards' said Bert. 'That runt Percy is causing so much misery and he doesn't even know it'

'I thought I was suffering' said Bert 'due to his bloody crows. So, what happened to the city manager.'

'You may have read the brief article that said he was leaving his post immediately as he had been offered a position out of the country. He was Australian and had contacts back there, I said he should take advantage and get out while he could as he couldn't hope to win fighting the cops. Hence the speedy departure. I was wondering if and when the cops would come after me as their net of blackmailees was starting to grow. However, it dawned on me they couldn't disclose my past, if they did then they would disclose theirs. It was status quo and much as I don't want to count my chickens, I am relatively safe.'

'But then you guys turn up'

'What if Percy told the cops about us.'

'Told the cops what about us.'

'Anything, how we got him drunk on Tom's deck'

'They would probably pat us on the back for that,' said Bert

'You know lot of this is starting to make sense,' said Tom.

'It's all bullshit,' said Bert. 'Think about it' said Tom, 'imagine, if Percy did go to the cops to tell them that we could provide information.'

'Information on what?' asked Tom.

'Hold on here, are you are assuming that Percy is just providing names to the cops for money or is he more devious and going after people that have wronged him. That's why we ended up at that meeting and Percy cleared off and left us to the cops. At the time' said Tom it all looked very innocent but the more you think about it, it hasn't been.'

'Actually, guys and Mr. Mayor, it's funny, Percy is a real gem, firstly he is conning the cops out of money and at the same time getting his revenge on us.'

'Don't you just love the guy' said Jim, 'I mean you two are meeting regularly with the cops and talking about the weather, food and goodness knows what expecting each other to fess up and pass on some appropriate information. You two have been dating for ages and you still haven't got each other into bed yet. I still think that the love birds had better call off this relationship before you two legends say something you shouldn't.'

'Ok, ok, you win Kev, we just want you to know that we enjoyed every moment of it while it lasted,' said Tom

'Sod me,' said Bert 'will we ever live this down.'

It was Friday afternoon, Tom walked in to Chat. Jim was stood at the bar chatting up a waitress, Tom left him to it and walked to the table.

'Heh Tom' called Charley from the back of the restaurant, 'how's things.?'

'Same old same old.'

Bert and Kev walked in.

Jim carried on chatting up the waitress.

Bert and Kev walked to the back of the restaurant, shook hands with Charley and looked over at Jim.

'It's a disease he has,' said Tom, 'I'm glad these two showed up otherwise I'd have been listening to Jim embarrassing the waitress or sat at our table talking to myself.'

'I'd have sat with you,' said Charley. 'Talking about your table, your friends came in yesterday and asked to sit at your table.'

'What friends' said Bert, 'we don't have any.'

'Those two guys Tom and Bert sat with last week.'

'Why purposely our table.'

'I believe I can answer that,' said Charley.

'Follow me and don't say a word.' They did as they were told.

They were at their table; Charley grabbed the edge and signaled Tom to help him flip it over. They stared at the underside of the table Charley pointed to a little black gizmo. They turned the table right way up, Charley put his finger to his lips and they followed him to the back of the restaurant.

'So, what's going on?' asked Jim.

'Go back to your lechering,' said Bert.

'Well,' said Jim ignoring Bert, 'it's a bug' said Charley.

'What a real one?' inquired Jim.

'I'm a bit of a routine freak' said Charley, 'every Friday I go around and tip a couple of the tables upside down and tighten the legs. It was your turn, I looked down at the underside of your table and there's this black thing, then it dawned on me; my cousin Rick amongst other things, is a PI, he has a couple of those things and has told me he can help me with one if I need it.'

'Rick popped round, took a look and warned me not to say anything near it. After he had taken another look, we went to the office at the back.

'He's funny is Rick, asked me what I had been up to, whose husband was after me.'

'I told the bozo that this was serious, how far away was it safe to talk.'

'Twenty feet is ok.'

The boys listened intently, for a change, as Charley filled them in.

'That's bizarre' said Kev, 'who are they trying to bug.'

'Obviously you,' said Charley

'It's too much of a coincidence. Two guys walk in and ask to sit at your table, the next day we find it bugged.'

'Maybe I'm a cynic' said Tom 'but it's too much of a coincidence, but then again, I'm sure that they were getting to the same state as we were. They were getting frustrated that they were getting nothing from us'

'That's wacky' said Bert 'in your position with something like that on you yet they come after us for making a few comments at a meeting, it doesn't make sense'

'We just have to make sure that the staff here know nothing of this. Ok Charley?'

'Ok'

The boys knew that they had to act as normal and natural as possible when seated at their table.

Over the next week they plotted and schemed the false information that they were going to feed the cops.

'I know we will talk about sport, sorry Jim, we know you won't be able to say too much, but then again you won't get us into trouble'

At the table the drinks arrived they chatted about how much the lottery was and paid their dues. They talked about Big Sam and little Sam which Jim hadn't a clue about and the waitress came over with another round, Jim was alright then he had somebody to talk to

They slipped away after a round of sambuca and Charley followed them outside. 'Thanks, my friend, be careful what you say near that table, but what about the customers sitting there said Bert.'

'Good point,' said Jim 'but you know the cops have to think that all is normal and if they eavesdrop on some tasty gossip then good luck to them.'

Let's think about what we are going to say and what seeds we are going to sow.

'Should we tell the Mayor about the bug or wait for the right time if that ever comes.'

'No, let's leave it for now,' said Tom, 'I still don't trust him, let's keep this in our back pocket'

The boys wracked their brains to think of a means and a way and what to say that would drop the cops in it. Over a beer in Kev's garden, they were still in doubt.

'Who can we mention so that we can build the story round them. Who do we want out of the way'

'There's the troll, there's the Mayor.'

'No, we need the Mayor' said Tom. Mary Moron,'

'I know' said Bert, 'what's his name from out east.'

'Yeah, but he's out of it and we want to let sleeping dogs lie.'

'I wonder if the Mayor would like somebody dropped in it.'

'Great but how would that work, he'll get suspicious'

'Hmmm, we need more beer to feed thought process'

'What's up with you' chuckled Bert,

'I was just laughing at us' said Jim. 'We should be lying on a beach somewhere, but here we are more stressed out than when we were working.

'I wouldn't call it stress' said Tom 'let's forget that and as we keep saying let's have some fun'

'Ok, let's just ad lib and see what happens, as you say let's have some fun,' said Tom.

'I like it' said Jim, 'in that way we will be more natural instead of trying to go from a script or trying to remember to fit all the bits together'

Friday afternoon, Tom was first there.
'Hi Charley,'

'Tom,' said Charley as they hugged. 'Have the deadly duo been in again' he asked.

'No, I guess the bug is still working or else they would have been by.'

'No doubt' said Tom, They must be having a good time listening to the table gossip and we will make sure that they have lots of entertainment later.'

Bert walked in shook hands with Charley,

'Ready Tom, ready Bert,'

They sat down at their table and their beers arrived.

Cheers' said Tom,

Kev arrived while Jim was still chatting to the lady behind the bar.

Normally they would have made comments about Jim and his antics with the women. However not today. They started chatting away about football in England, this must have been really entertaining for the cops.

'Come to join us have you Jim,' said Kev.

Ignoring them Jim had a sip of his beer,

'Hey I was talking to this guy at the golf club today, the head pro there is pretty sick, they don't think he will make it.'

'How old is he?' said Bert

'Isn't he mid-fifties Jim' asked Kev.

'Yeah, and a good guy' said Jim,

'Why is that crooks survive and the good guys go early.'

'Yeah' said Kev 'Talking about golf, did you hear about that little cop in his golf buggy, I don't know what he carries in it or where he goes when he drives through the bushes.'

Tom gave Kev a smile and a thumb's up. 'I've heard he's got quite the home, car, and all the toys, not bad on a cop's pay.'

What the cops on the other end of the bug couldn't see were the smiling faces of the guys and them high fiving each other.

'We should arrange a meeting with our friends, but do you think that they would want to know that kind of stuff?' said Tom.

'If they don't they will soon tell you,' said Kev.

'Talking about sport Tom, the biggest joke is the sports club,' said Bert. I've been thinking about it for a long time. How do they get away with charging the parents of 5-year old's $200 for a total of 5/6 sessions, less if it's raining? There is no proper instruction, it is done by parents who have paid for the right to teach their kids about something they know nothing about. Imagine 10 teams, 15 kids a team times $200, that's $30,000, not bad. Run this through the whole enterprise, why do the kids have to do bottle drives etc. don't forget that's the lower end, there are parents paying out far more than $200 per kid.'

'So where does the money go?' asked Tom.

Well, they can pay a bunch of staff exorbitant wages for what little they do and the committee members can sneak off to the best hotels for a glitzy weekend disguised as a meeting

'Love it,' mouthed Jim and they all high fived yet again.

Another round arrived.

'So, what are you up to this weekend' Jim asked the waitress.

'I'll be working here' she said.

'That's a shame.'

'Jim, her boyfriend is six four and amongst other things is a linebacker for the university,'

'I am not interested in him,' said Jim.

'You would have more chance with him than her,' said Tom.

'Listen you, I'm making real progress, last week she was ignoring me, now she's insulting me.'

The repartee continued, the sambuca's came and went and they sneaked out the door with a wave to Charley.

'I thought that that went great' said Jim as they walked down the street. 'By the way, where did the bit about the bimbo in the golf cart come from?'

'I don't know' said Kev, 'I can't stand him and everybody you talk to thinks he's a jerk. Hopefully they check him out and eventually he will lose his buggy, they will arrest him or whatever.'

'I wonder how they will feel about the sports thing, we had better arrange the meeting to find out' said Tom

The boys were having a beer on Bert's deck, his phone rang.

'Charley, how are you?.... no!'

'I guess they'd had enough of listening to us, what a shame we could have put together something better for the next show, great and thanks Charley see you soon.'

The boys met as usual Friday.

'Don't worry' said Charley I re checked under the table, it's gone.

That wasn't good enough for Jim, he was on his hands and knees looking up at the underside of the table.

What's up with him said the waitress.

'Don't ask, we think he's found religion,' said a resigned Bert. 'Get up in case you spill the beer then you will be in trouble.'

What's the plan when you meet your friends next week

'Well, I reckon that we ease gently into the cop in the buggy scenario, see how that goes and then go for the sports jugular' said Tom

The boys were still in experimental mode. They knew they needed something cheap and nasty something easy that they could get involved in that won't cause them to give anything away.

'What about the road works.'

'No better not, suppose as we think the Mayor is up to no good and there is fraud. One big investigation and the Mayor is thrown out of power or in jail without us being able to milk him and the system'

'There has to be a hint of corruption, that's why the sports club is perfect. Too much and it becomes like a telegraphed pass, easy to pick up on'

The cops were already sat at the boys table in Chat when Tom and Bert arrived. They started off as usual talking about the weather.

'Any good arrests lately' smirked Tom, there wasn't even a snigger. Bert thought to himself that humor wasn't big with these two. He was also wondering how they ended up doing what they were doing. Obviously, it wasn't an official role, these two were just out to make a few extra dollars on the side

'Do you ever get issues where cops are milking the system,' said Tom.

'What do you mean by that' said Al the bigger of the two.

'Well one of the things that comes up time after time around the neighborhood is your buddy on the golf buggy.'

'What about him.'

'Well,' said Bert there are stories about him wandering the trails and trees with stuff in the back of his buggy.'

'What kind of stuff?' asked Al.

'Now these are only rumors' said Bert stirring the pot 'but one guy said he had it on good authority that he was delivering booze.'

'Booze' said Al 'to who.'

'That's all we know, won't take you guys long to confirm that, will it?'

They sensed things were going well, Tom gave the nod to Bert who brought up the fact that the other thing that bothers a lot of people is whether there is corruption at the sports club.

'What are you on about, that seems a bit far fetched.'

'As we had it put to us; how do they get away with charging parents of 5-year-olds $200 for a total of 5/6 sessions in the spring, even less if raining. There is no proper instruction, it is done by parents who have paid for the right to teach their kids about something they know nothing about. Imagine, 10 teams 15 kids a team times $200, that's $30,000, not bad. Run this through the whole enterprise. Why do the kids have to do bottle drives etc. don't forget that's the lower end, many parents are paying out far more than $200 per kid. Where does the money go? We've been told that they pay a bunch of staff exorbitant wages for what little they do and so the committee members can sneak off to five-star resort hotels for a glitzy weekend disguised as a meeting or so-called coaching session in the US or Europe.'

Bert carried on, 'When was the last time a team from here won anything. Where does the money go, they should be extending the sports academies to give every kid a chance to play at their best level for as little cost as possible.'

'Most of the sports are elitist. The reason that the city has never been successful or produced quality athletes is because only the rich can play. The next super star could be here but they can't play for a top team with its fancy outfits, equipment, trips etc. simply because the parents to can't afford it. It's sad

'Your little one goes to the sports club doesn't he, said Dennis, looking at Al, 'how many sessions does he play in the summer?'

'About five.'

'How much did you pay,'

'About 240.'

'You are right in what you are saying said Al, 'My wife tells me all the time it's a waste of damn money.'

'Who coached them.'

'I wouldn't call it coaching because Aidan's dad was seconded into coaching at the last minute to coach the kids. Then at the first practice he got another couple of parents to volunteer because without them there would be no sports for the kids.'

'Well what sports coaching experience or sports knowledge do these guys have.'

'Absolutely none.'

'So where does the money go?

'Good point.'

Tom smiled at Bert

'How many teams are there.'

'I don't know but guessing 6.'

'So that's $18,000'

'$18,000 rents a lot of fields in the summer over just a 6-week period'

'Yes, there are lots of other teams taking part in different activities, but the principle's the same, tons of money produced from parents of kids who are just fodder and a mechanism to provide a bunch of egotistical people with jobs, a means to fund their sports and social activities elitist so called representative teams.'

The boys had really hit a nerve, Tom and Bert sat back and listened as Al took over.

'These kids aren't necessarily the best players of their age groups in the City. They are mainly there because most sports are financially elitist, their parents pay out large amounts of money each year for fees, kit, balls, travel, hotels, tournaments etc. so that they can say that their son(s) or daughter(s) play for the City rep team. Consequently, even more money goes into the club's coffers.'

'Not that I know too much about too many sports' said Dennis 'but I stand there listening to other parents, especially those with older kids. You know what the biggest moan is. It's about referees.'

'You have to have them,' said Tom.

'Agreed, said Al 'but why do they get paid and coaches don't.'

'The coaches put in far more time than referees.   One guy was telling me that at a soccer game he was at, the referee was so fat he couldn't run and never made it out of the center circle the whole game. He was actually paid for that'

'The fields look good; they do and should do, they are hardly used, a slight sprinkling of rain and the kids aren't allowed to use them. That's ridiculous, if that was Britain and you couldn't play in the rain then nobody would ever play sport. It's a shame, the kids might get dirty, the referees wet, while the well-paid staff sit in the bar.'

'Then the staff go on "trips" to Europe and or the U.S. to learn about various sports. These trips are paid for out of the fees that the 5-year-old kids parents pay so that their 5-year-old kids can have a run around on a summers evening.'

'Exactly,' said Bert, 'all this experience that the staff and committee members somehow learn must be imparted somewhere somehow. One of the coaches, a friend of mine, was told that he had been selected to go to a sports clubs' association meeting, he was over the moon. He thought it would be at a local sports club premises. Oh no it was held at one of the biggest and best hotels. He was picked up at the door, flown to the nearest airport, driven to the hotel, on the Friday. There was a meeting on the Saturday morning after breakfast. Then lunch a free afternoon before the big banquet with wine etc. and drinks afterwards. Breakfast Sunday morning, driven to airport flown back and driven home all at the expense of the parents' fees for grass roots sports'

'You know all this and haven't said anything about it.'

Dennis was dismayed at what was happening at the sports club with the local kids not being given the chance to play and develop their sports skills. He was looking forward to investigating the goings on there and saw it as an opportunity not only to change things, but make charge the management a fee for their version of business interruption insurance.

Gentlemen we appreciate you telling us this. We will update you as we check these things out. It may take some time.

The cops picked up the tab and the four of them got up to leave.

'Stay in touch and if there's anything we can do for you or help you with let us know.'

Bert and Tom waived as the cops drove away.

'You know Tom, whether there is corruption or not, the people who run sports club are only in it for their own ends. I have a feeling that those two will be doing some investigations with a view to making a few dollars.'

They walked round the block and back into Chat

Well, my friends, how was it' said Charley.

'Good' said Tom, 'I think that we got our points across.'

They didn't want to say too much as Charley was on the board of the sports club.

15.

Nicely relaxed, beer at hand, comfortable surroundings. 'Now we have lawyers in place we need a good firm of accountants, said Tom.

'What about the guy I use,' said Jim

'You must be on a different bloody planet' said Bert, 'everybody knows the guy is a dickhead, him doing your personal taxes once a year Jim doesn't make him an accountant and let's face it you are always moaning about him. Your only criteria is that he is cheap,'

'I know he's cheap' added Jim.

'Yeah, but that's your main criteria for everything', interrupted Bert 'and you get what you pay for'

They had all heard bits about him and none of it was good.

'How did you find him, was he hiding under a rock.' asked Tom.

'We met at the golf club,'

'Surprise, surprise said Kev,

Ignoring him, Jim told them that he joined a foursome that was one short,

'I must admit I didn't like him one bit, you know you can tell if a player is useful, but he was crap, he kept telling us he was having a bad day. By the time we got to about the sixteenth I was learning that the other two were taking him for a game much to suck up to him as he was a client. We ended up in the bar and after one drink the two guys said they had to go; I could sense their relief when they left by themselves.

He sat with Archie quite stunned and at an impasse. He wasn't ready to go as long as somebody else was picking up the tab. We should have another one said Archie, but of course he wasn't a member and guess who was on the hook.'

'After another drink he started to open up, how he had started off as an accountant' said Jim 'working for a large accountant doing audits and such like.

'Don't tell me he thought that that was boring.' said Kev

'Have you finished?' asked a ticked off Jim.

'Hey Kev, did you know he's been married three times. He really liked discussing his wives. The first one was a real bitch, the second one was a drunk and dumb, she couldn't fit in to his new environment as the president of a company, in the end she told him that she had had enough of him.'

'Gee he admitted that said Kev.'

'Well by then he was getting pretty loaded. Then he decided to go on line.'

'You're kidding' said Tom 'what did he end up with.

'A dermatologist from somewhere in Europe,'

'He certainly goes all in doesn't he.'

'You gotta believe it', said Jim, 'I didn't know whether to laugh or cry. She talked him into going on a trip to Europe. She had lots of money and he had to go to see cultural things like museums, churches and palaces he was way out of his social and comfort zone. He watched her buy expensive clothes and jewelry, while he was paying for the trip. In the end she dumped him.'

'You can imagine it said Kev sounds like he was way out of his depth.'

'So then, there's more,' asked Tom.

'Oh yeah, we didn't get out of there till past midnight. It was like I was his psychologist, he needed somebody to talk to, I am sure that he was introverted and must be a really lonely person. I felt so sorry for him, that's why he does my taxes.'

'Oh, big deal' said Tom 'you are all heart and he's cheap'

'So, what about the next one?' asked Kev.

'Oh, she was different and not just her nationality' said Jim,

'He was going through the nations of the world,' said Bert.

'Oh, this is the funniest yet. It appears that the ladies he goes with are ok but he takes things so seriously and is so insecure he changes his lifestyle, to be compatible with the particular woman's heritage, he figures that will make them like him and be compatible. Whatever she tells him about lifestyle he believes. He started giving me a lecture on herbal medicine, which he became an expert on while he was on a two-week holiday with her. He now figures that that is the best country in the world to live in.'

'What I can't understand and I bet you didn't ask him, is if that country is so great why are they still living here?' said Tom.

'You are right, but I didn't get a chance because he was then right into a lecture on how bad dairy products are for me.'

'And you want him to be our accountant Jim, you are a prick,' said Bert.

'Yeah, but he's cheap' laughed Jim

'So how did he become an accountant again.'

'Well obviously they eventually realized what an idiot he was and retired him early. By then he wasn't making a lot of sense so I packed him in a cab and sent him home.'

'Bert,' said Tom, 'you know our lawyers really well, pick their brains for an accountancy firm and see if they can get us a good deal.'

The following week, the boys and their lawyer were introduced to their accountants. The accountants were pretty shell shocked when they heard what the boys were involved in.

'You should have come to us earlier' said Grenville,

'We've been too busy and don't forget we are retired,' said Tom.

'All right, all right' he said 'I get it'.

Why don't accountants have a sense of humor whispered Kev, I bet Jim doesn't get this hassle from Archie

You know who used to work for Archie' said Jim, 'Peter. The guy who was a real good friend of yours' Bert.

'Yeah right,' said Bert.

Jim used to give Bert a hard time, because Peter was pretty good at embellishing the truth and used to tell Jim that he was a partner of Bert's and Bert used to come to Pete all the time for advice.

"You prick" said Bert to Jim

According to Pete, Archie had heard of Pete's reputation and wanted a top man to run a department. Pete tells the story that he kept turning the job down until he got the perfect deal.

'You want to hear his stories especially about how he was a partner of yours and taught you everything you know'

What's Pete doing now 'said Bert,

'Why, do you want to get together with him, for old times' sake and get some advice,' said Jim.

'Sod off' whispered Bert.

'I am sure that like the rest of us, he's retired.
'

16.

All of a sudden there was a tremendous amount of construction going on in and around the City, curiosity became prevalent.

Seeing the various projects starting up created growing interest as to what was happening. People were more concerned about what was imminent, rather than what was behind the projects

Word on the street was rife. The boys' neighbors had had letters from the city as part of the planning process.

Jim was out in the street talking to a guy he knew, who lived around the corner. He and a couple of his neighbors had been down to the city to see the plans. Personally, we don't mind as we are far enough away, the fact that vehicles won't be allowed to park really helps as we are getting fed up with people parking outside our homes anyway. A works bus picks up workers around the corner, if they want to catch a work bus they really don't care where they park so having neighborhood restricted parking will be great. What a lot of the people around here like is that we will be living in a vineyard with a coffee shop and nice restaurant as part of our neighborhood, just like the complex down the road. If only the city could do something with downtown.

As they were talking Gladys whose house would be directly overlooked by the condo walked by. I was thinking of selling and buying a condo as I really don't need this big house. I am not happy she said having a big condo in my back yard. I mean what's it going to do to the value of my house.

'Gladys, I've an idea' said Jim, 'how about a condo in the new development, you could stay amongst your friends and neighbors. You would have the vineyard over the road, coffee shops, restaurants boutiques, the river valley down the road and downtown fifteen minutes' walk away'

The penny dropped with Gladys; she was thrilled. All of a sudden Jim was being peppered with questions about the condominium. She was soon telling her friends and neighbors which helped with the consent.

The boys, the project manager and the Mayor were at Chat when Jim walked in.

'You are late,' said Bert.

'Some of us have been working' he smiled.

'Yeah right' said Tom 'game took longer than you thought.'

'You are talking to the salesman of the month; I have just sold a condo. He told them the story.

'You know the good thing' said Tom, 'Gladys will be telling the neighborhood her good news.'

'Where are we at with our projects' said Bert.

'Well,' said the Mayor, 'the council will vote in favor, but there is an agitator.'

'Don't say the tree huggers are back at it.'

'No problem there' said the mayor, 'they have enough on their plates what with some of them visiting the stocks and law suits flying around'

'Actually, you know him quite well. He's your next-door neighbor Bert.'

'Who Percy.'

'Yes', said the Mayor. 'He's the self-styled vigilante of the neighborhood.'

'I knew there was a reason why I didn't like the guy,' said Jim. 'Look at when Tom and Bert went to the meeting at the cop shop with him, what a disaster.'

'But he was telling me he was looking at moving into a senior's place' said Bert, 'so why would he resent the development. '

'Well,' said the Mayor, 'he feels that the neighborhood should stay the same.'

'That illustrates what a prick he is said Bert, what does he care. he wants to sell and move away'

'I told you he was a nut case,' said Jim.

'So, what about an update on our projects'

'Well said the project manager, as you can see the re construction of your road has been completed up to where the condo and vineyard start,'

'All necessary planning has been approved for demolition of your properties the continued development of the vineyard, the parking lots, the river valley and downtown.'

'It's going to take anywhere from three to six months to finalize the financing, legal, marketing etc. but there are bits we can do. The vineyard for instance has already been planted, the river had to be attended to after the spill so we used the Government money to clean up and for soft costs for the development of the dam and canal.

The Mayor's good friend out east, after a few legal conversations, threats of media reaction and a small settlement decided to relinquish his rights to ownership in favor of the city

'What about the newspaper' said the project manager

'Looking good' said Tom, 'we or should I say Henry is now managing it for us. We are working on a media campaign to introduce all of the projects. In fact, the Mayor is even more popular than ever.'
Jim stuck a finger down his throat

Bert went to see Percy and explained, how beneficial the condo was to the neighbourhood and that holding it up now would put many of his neighbours' futures in jeopardy.

'I see what you mean about having a unit in the building Bert' said Percy, 'but if you don't mind, I still want a unit in the senior's place up the road.'

That's your decision Percy as long as you are happy.' said Bert not so sure that he meant it.

'I do have a major fear' and that is said Bert trying hard to be empathetic, 'How can I sell my house with that development going up next door.'

'I know a couple of people involved in the development of the condominium and will have words' said Bert 'but I am sure that the condo development company will help you out and buy your house.' Bert didn't want to say too much as Percy might get wind that they needed the land for the condominium.

'That's really good of you Bert,' said Percy

Anything to get rid of you, you eccentric arsehole thought Bert.

Within a couple of weeks, the whole side of the road, had been acquired with the residents selling to the City and happy to buy a condo unit.

A couple of residents over the road from the development appealed, but of course lost.

The vineyard condo development started, the houses were demolished, the number of people taking a look at the area was extraordinary. The newspaper was doing a fantastic job in presenting the condo units, in fact one could say that there was substantial interest in the development

The locals were getting first chance at the units in the six-storey building with the boys having a top floor penthouse each.

It was spring. Across the road and kitty corner from the condo the vines were starting to bud. The cold harsh winter never really materialized so with work on the condominium moving along, the vineyard shops, coffee shop and restaurant were all taking shape.

With the snow gone, the sunshine now bringing warmth, flocks of people and nosey neighbors were buzzing around the fenced off site. The condo show studio was really busy, in fact so busy entrance was by appointment only. Within weeks the majority of the condos were sold

'You know' said Jim, in-between swallows of beer sat at their table in Chat, we should have got the coffee shop open straight away we'd have made a killing, Good point said Tom but it would be a zoo there, people treading over the building site and the vines. Let's get it finished. Quite honestly, I'm in favor of getting the condo finished first, moving in, making sure that the vines are looked after and the road and pathways complete.

'I can't wait to get on the roof and see the view across the river valley described Kev. Think about it, there will be no cars, we will have access at the side directly into the underground parking lot. Even visitors to the residents will park underground.'

'I must admit the owners of the plaza up the road weren't too happy when they were approached by the City about building a bus drop off and pick up point at the edge of its parking lot. However, when it was explained to them the increase in foot traffic of visitors walking past the stores in the plaza, their eyes lit up.'

'Nevertheless,' said Jim, 'if they hadn't of liked it, would it have mattered'

'I am sure the city would have dealt with that in our favor' said Bert as he signalled to the bar for another round.

So, there it was, either you parked and walked or parked and took the special bus, the boys were happy though that once the novelty had worn off, the vineyard would be an idyllic spot to have a spot of lunch, dinner or just a drink.

Rodney and Gareth were thrilled at the way the vines were coming along and more so their little purpose-built barn, the future home of Mere Folly wines. Gareth especially, an engineer and inventor, was having a great time kitting out the winery.

17.

The editorial in the newspaper boosted local interest in all the construction projects underway in the city. It explained how lucky the citizens were to have a council that supported the redevelopment. In addition, there was a supplement detailing the new projects and what could be expected.

The majority were amazed as plans, renderings and schematics illustrated, the new river valley parkway, the vineyard center, the vineyard condominium, the parking lots, free shuttle service and the downtown redevelopment. There was also some astonishment when it was announced that the traffic circle to nowhere was being torn up

An e mail to the editor asking that the name not be published chastised the council on its reckless spending and that taxes would go through the roof. An article appeared the following week explaining that taxes would actually go down and that all future projects would be subsidized from the income derived from tourism and new business taxes coming to the city.

Whilst the writer of the e mail's name was not published, upon "investigation" it was discovered that he was an anarchist and involved in the pollution of the river incident. His name was passed on to the friendly cops who eventually increased their income by digging up some dirt on him and charged him a fee to keep it hushed up. Most people would call it blackmail but the cops called it business interruption insurance. Strange, but his hobby of anarchy ceased.

The river was temporarily dammed, drained and the new pumping station built. Residents came and watched as day by day the parkway and the river /canal took shape. Downtown was a major construction site.

Businesses were complaining about having to work in the middle of a construction site and pay exorbitant taxes. The exodus to the outskirts was starting. Not that the outskirts were that far away from downtown. Office centers on the outskirts of the city had zero vacancy rates and new buildings were starting to spring up, filled by lawyers, doctors and insurance brokers trying to escape from the purgatory of operating downtown. The downtown area was blending in with the river parkway.

The boys always looked forward to their relaxing beer on Friday afternoon, listening to the gossip, peoples' ideas of what was happening and going on, rumors were rife.

Charley didn't bother them too much, although there was always a free sambuca at the end of their session. As Bert said, 'a couple of years ago we never got a free drink, but now you can tell he senses that there's something in the offing and wants a return for services rendered'

'Hey, hey,' said Jim, 'look who's walked in now.'

The boys had known Mario many years, their common language was football, perhaps that's why Jim had nothing to do but chat up the waitresses while the Europeans discussed the beautiful game.

'I hear that you guys have moved into the development business and not small stuff either.' Said Mario joining them at their table. He had every right to as he owned Chat and another ten restaurants,

They knew it, there had to be a reason why he would pop in and immediately sit with them at this time on a Friday.

'Goodness me, where did you hear that Mario, can't four old retired guys have a hobby,' said Tom

The waiter wandered over with a tray of GM's, Tom winked at Bert and Jim and whispered to Bert, what's he after.

After the usual football chat where as usual Bert was on the receiving end as his team was a pretty easy target, Mario bid his farewells. He suggested that they pop down to his head office the coming week. 'Love to talk to you about your project, how about Wednesday 11.30, we can chat in private.'

That's Mario, he hasn't got where he has through messing about, right to the point. They knew what he wanted; they glanced around to make sure nobody was eavesdropping.' They were sure he will want to get involved in the venture especially the restaurants and other foodie things. The boys had no objection, but in moderation, they wanted the food, beverage facilities to be as diverse as possible and top notch. They were positive about the need to create a foodie paradise, not necessarily expensive restaurants but really good quality places,

Back to Mario, they needed him. 'Let's face it, we want quality, therefore you have to work with the best. That's why we need Mario, to help us on the food stuff and beverage stuff, but we should only allow him a couple of spots. If we give him more, he will be taking over the whole food enterprise.' Said Kev

For once they agreed with the Mayor when he said and the whole council agreed, "the city isn't in the design and construction business", therefore it appointed a consultancy company, that happened to be owned by the boys to oversee the whole umbrella. The city didn't have to pay this company, it just shared in any ongoing profit. The holding company set up other companies to actually operate the various entities such as leasing downtown store space, leasing space along the river, operating the parking lots, food and beverage, functions in the city. The shuttle buses will be free with the expense of running the service picked up by advertising, guide books and food and beverage services.

The boys sat in Mario's board room with Mario and a couple of his team.

'Nice room,' said Jim.

Mario thanked them for coming in a kind of cold clinical way. 'I understand that you are involved in developing your small city. Correct me if I'm wrong but I thought that you guys had retired, so what are you up to?'

They explained to Mario that three of them had had cancer operations, were getting bored, saw that the city was dying on its feet under the control of a bent Mayor and a demented council. They also had the opinion that they hadn't long left anyway, so decided what the heck, they should have some fun and get their city back

'Very noble,' said Mario.

'You always were a bit of a prick Mario,' said Bert. 'You dragged us here. Enough of the niceties, what do you want?'

'As I said, I understand that you will need restaurants and pubs, in a nutshell, food establishments I would like to set up as many as you need.'

'Perfect,' said Kev 'every other building will be an Italian restaurant.'

'What's up with that laughed Mario, I can just see it, little Italy in Mere Folly or, as I hear you are building a canal, what about little Venice' In all seriousness guys, how long have we known each I would love to work with you.'

'We would love to work with you Mario' said Tom, 'but a couple of your type of establishments would be adequate. What we envision is a range of quality restaurants and eateries. There are plenty of fast-food places in other parts of the city, if that's what people want. In addition, they aren't too far from the river parkway and downtown core.'

'So, what do you want me to do?' asked Mario.

'Just what we asked,' Kev confirmed, 'use your expertise to help the architect, designer plan, review applicants, due diligence, construct and operate, the food and beverage side of the development.'

'Great let's arrange meetings with your key people, James here is head of my construction and renovation division we will get him involved.'

'Hold on, hold on,' said Tom. 'We already have the people on board to project manage the construction. No disrespect James but we don't need you, hopefully Mario does.'

'Well, if James and my construction division aren't involved then nor am I.'

'Don't get bent out of shape, you are missing the point Mario,' said Bert, 'we already have our people in place to project manage and construct. In fact, they are well into the various projects. If you want James to help with your position as a consultant on this project no problem, you might need him.'

Mario's ego was severely dented both from a personal and financial aspect as initially he could see a great opportunity to make money, not just as a consultant but from the disproportionate and excessive profits and backhanders from sub-contractors etc.

Kev, after being deep in thought on the way back to Mere Folly suddenly said, 'how well do Charley and Mario know each other.'

'Cousins' said Bert,

'Shit' said Kev.

'What's the matter?' asked Tom.

'Pretty obvious how Mario found out about us being in the development business as he put it and going forward, he'll blab about the cops, especially as he knows so much and especially if the cops go after the sports club and its board members.'

'We didn't exactly leave Mario in good spirits either did we. I wonder about Charley' said Tom, 'like we've always said, trust no one, but the more expansive we get we have to draw people into our confidence.'

'Yeah, but that's our weak link 'added Kev. 'I think we should have a chat with Charley, but let's leave it until next Friday as he might find it strange if we descend upon him and start quizzing him. I wonder if he knows we met with Mario. Between now and then we can give some thought to how we approach him.'

'No' said Tom, 'the more you plan and script, the more plastic it will appear. Let's just ad lib and see if we can figure out whether there is anything that we should be concerned about.'

During the week Mario was trying to get hold of Bert, but Bert didn't want to talk any more with him until he had chatted with Charley.

Tom and Jim arrived at Chat first, sat down and waited for their beer, the other two arrived shortly after.

'So how do we start?' asked Kev.

'I think we just ask him if he has heard or seen the cops' said Tom and take it from there. We'll wing it'.

Their second beers arrived, 'Where's Charley,' said Jim to the waitress

'He's left.'

'Already, the days only just begun,' said Bert. 'Is he coming back later?'

'No, he's left, gonzo, quit'.

'You what' said Bert spilling his beer down his shirt and wiping the beer from his mouth.

'Where's he gone, has he got another job'.

'Don't know.'

'Is that your line or the official line,' said Tom.

'No honest said the waitress, I don't know, he was her one minute and then gone. Claudio, Mario's son came in and told us on Wednesday that Charley wouldn't be back. He said he had decided to leave and wouldn't be back.'

'Sod me,' said Bert

Just then who should come in the back door but Mario.

'Now we can ask the big guy,' said Bert.

Eventually, after talking to some of his staff and the odd customer, Mario made his way to the boys table. Drawing up another chair, he sat down. 'I've been trying to get hold of you Bert most of the week.'

'How come' said Bert, 'By the way what happened to Charley.'

'That's why I was chasing you.'

'That bastard has been fiddling me. Family bloody fiddling family, can you believe it.'

He shut up as his drink arrived.

As soon as the waitress left Mario was straight into it again.

'Can you believe it, he was fiddling his own family. You know what he was doing, he was pinching the food from the cafe.'

'No' said Tom quite unaffectedly.

'We thought the place was doing great with the food that he was ordering but the receipts didn't match,' said an upset Mario

'How could he be fiddling,' said Jim, acting dumb, 'when he owned fifty percent of the business.'

'You what' said Mario, 'who told you that.'

'He did.'

'Do you think I would give Charley fifty percent of a new enterprise like this,'

'No' said Bert 'we thought that it was strange, you giving anything away, he told us he had bought in.'

'Bought in said a distraught Mario, getting madder and madder. He hadn't got two dimes to rub together. I gave him the job up there and then down here because he was family.'

Tom beckoned Mario to calm down as he was getting louder and louder

Mario's voice slowed and softened, 'and this is what he does to me.'

'What are you going to do about him?' asked Kev.

'I was stupid in more ways than one. When I had checked the receipts on Monday, I told him they weren't making sense and I would be over Tuesday to sort it out. I should have just gone straight over and not told him I was coming.'

'When I got here Tuesday, I waited, but he didn't show so I phoned. No answer. Then I went over to the place he was renting. No answer. I couldn't get into his apartment, but its like he's just disappeared.'

'Surprise, surprise,' said Kev, 'what are you going to do.'

'Not much I can do is there'.

'What about the cops.'

'What's the point, there's no real evidence, they are not going to search for him and he's still family. Besides I don't need this getting out there.'

The boys smiled at each other, more or less in relief than anything, as each of them was thinking, if not saying, that with Charley gone, and hopefully disappeared off the face of the earth, they had dodged another bullet.

'Well,' said Tom, 'its no use moping Mario, life goes on and we haven't got a lot of it left.'

'At this rate' said Mario 'you'll outlive me no problem, but you are right let's get on with our project.'

'So, you are in?'

'Get some ideas mapped out Mario, lets meet here this time next week.'

'Ok' said Mario 'and by the way start thinking of what's in it for me. I have to get some money back now I have been robbed.'

'Bloody typical' said Bert, 'see you next week.'

As they were finishing their drinks, Mario left through the back door. 'Well, we might as well discuss what we do next,' said Kev as he signaled for another round and carried on.

'I thought you guys were off' said Claudio, 'bringing some customers to their table.'

'Tough' said Kev, getting the evil eye, 'that kid needs to grow up. Thinks he owns the place already. Good job he wasn't around when Charley was distributing the stock'.

'Phew that could have been nasty.' Said Jim

'Nasty' said Bert 'notwithstanding Charley's grocery business, if he'd have spoken to our friendly cops, or blabbed about our relationship with the cops, it could have been a real mess.'

'Especially if the cops investigated him and the board at the sports club,' went on Tom. 'At least we can sit and watch the carnage when those two start their blackmail scheme'

The boys were convinced that it will make interesting reading in their newspaper in due course

'What do we do about Mario and how do we pay him?'

'Well talking about the newspaper, we can offer to pay all his advertising costs. He needn't know that we own the paper.'

'Great idea, so what other options do we have available that we can offer?' Asked Jim.

'There could be free rent because obviously there will be no ownership of the premises,' suggested Tom.

'That's a bit rich,' said Jim.

'I'm still laughing at Charley and his ownership of this place; I thought Mario was going to have a heart attack,' said Bert.

'Why not?' asked Tom

'Why not what?' asked Bert.

'Why not ask for 51% of this place, he does the consultancy work, gets a very large fee and gets free rent for two establishments.'

18.

Over the weekend they chatted backwards and forwards while their wives were getting frustrated.

'You were retiring so that we could spend more time together, travel a bit and relax. All you seem to be doing is going off to Chat for a beer.' Ranted Bert's wife.

'They just don't get it do they, here we are trying to build something to give us all a new lease on life for that bit of life we have left and all that happens is we get is nagged to death. Perhaps we should lie on the couch and watch tv all day, now that would really give them something to nag about.'

Having let off steam, Bert continued, 'more importantly, how do we sort out Mario.' The boys were trying to decide on how much they should tell him.

'Firstly, we tell him nothing' said Bert 'remember our pledge when we first chatted. We have fallen off the log a couple of times and it's nearly cost us.'

'Yes, but we do have to sort him out one way or another.' Replied Jim. 'What do we give him and what do we take in return.'

'We are getting nowhere, let's bring in the expertise, let's talk to the accountants and lawyers.'

'That will cost us' said Jim.

'You bozo,' said Tom 'It could cost us a heck of a lot more if we don't do it right.'

'The accountants crunched the numbers and between them and the boys, they conjured up a proposal for a deal.'

'Ok Mario,' said Bert as they sat in Mario's board room, we've had discussions with our lawyers and accountants.'

'You're coming in with the heavy artillery interrupted Mario.'

'No, we are doing it sensibly and properly so that it's beneficial to us all. What's the point of a year down the road if one of us is upset about a deal gone wrong because it wasn't scoped adequately'

Mario listened to the proposition and then asked them what alternative he had.

'None really said Bert, 'but we think it is fair to all parties.' Bert went on to explain that the accountants and lawyers had done a good job, "If you can think of something better.'

'Interesting, proposition,' said a pensive Mario.

There was silence as the boys waited for the counter or for Mario just to get up and walk away.

'I appreciate the work and expense that you have gone to, but; shit thought Bert, then Mario smiled, "I'll pass your proposal on to my heavy artillery, we have a deal.'

They all shook hands, out came the aperitifs to cement the deal and off they went to Mario's flagship restaurant. A taxi was needed to get them home deep in the knowledge that they had a consultant on board and a majority share in their Friday afternoon lair.

Mario was true to his word and by the time Friday rolled round the paperwork had arrived back at the lawyers.

'We had better explain to our wives what we've done,' said Kev.

'Oh shit,' said Bert. 'How are we going to explain this without telling them too much.'

'Why not invite them down to Chat this afternoon, said Kev. 'We can tell them and its partly true, that Mario wanted to open a restaurant and consult for us so he gave us a piece of the café in return.'

The boys thought that it was a great idea, although the wives were a little dubious. There were some caustic comments as they arrived and settled down.

'I hear that congratulations are in order,' said Claudio as he arrived with the boy's beer and a bottle of champagne.

'Congratulations, exclaimed Rita,' Bert's wife, 'what have you clowns been up to now'.

'Well, hesitated Tom, 'we decided we were spending too much money here so we decided to buy the place.'

You could have cut the air with a knife; certain people were not exactly pleased. If there was a time to push for a divorce, this was it.

'You told us in no uncertain terms that we are not too good at communicating'.

'Hold on a minute said Deidre, it's alright communicating after you are involved in one of your brilliant schemes but what about bringing us into your confidence and asking our advice prior to.'

The boys went through the canned version of the deal that they had put together with Mario, what it involved, the benefits and then explained the rationale behind the purchase of Chat. Despite this the evening was rather subdued. The only consolation was that there was no bill.

As Bert said, when they next got together, "that's the last sodding time".

Despite the fact that they had achieved miracles, there was no appreciation and decided that the pledge now included their wives.

They were hoping that the design portfolio for the condo and some of the buildings and the landscaping they had entrusted to them with would keep them happy and out of their hair.

In the week that followed they met with Henry at the newspaper. Revenue was up especially advertising, Henry had thought of hiring a rep to go out and beat the bushes, but with the introductions that the boys were presenting there was a steady flow of advertising in the door. Of course, having heard on the rumor mill of the new developments taking place, a lot of the business came from entities that wanted to suck up. The boys laughed at the thought that they were encouraging advertising in the paper whereas a year ago they were the first to complain about the local rag just being an adverting broadsheet with very little news content.

'How the cookie crumbles,' Jim speculated.

The city always looks rather desolate, in winter. Looking at travel brochures the tourist always visualizes thee area from the perspective of the glamour of snow in the mountains and pristine frozen rivers which paints a picture of beauty. This may be so in the mountains, but of course this is not reality in the cities, towns and villages. With a combination of snow and mud, commonly known to the locals as snud, everywhere looked dirty. Vehicles on the road looked like blobs of grey concrete. Wherever you went, stores, restaurants, homes dirt is dragged in with you as you tramp through the snud. One wondered, looking at the mess how it could ever be cleared up.

Within a month or so give or take the odd snowfall and or temperature dip, the warmth came back, the snow and ice went, the snud was cleaned up and the cities, towns and villages gleamed again. Overnight, fields went through a colour change, from white to brown to green and yellow. Nature at its finest.

So, it was in Mere Folly, despite the cold desolation of winter, construction had started on the various developments. The pump station and water controls for the new river / canal system had been completed prior to winter. Downtown was looking pretty desolate as many of the office buildings were empty although as they emptied the basic renovations started.

The realty division was busy talking to potential store and business owners. After pre-qualification and due diligence, they were put in touch with the planners and designers.

More importantly, the farmers market, that was nearly history as the council under pressure from the suits in the office buildings, didn't like the congestion around their premises.

Now, you have to understand the mentality of these idiots, who mostly didn't live in the city or even visit the city except to work. The market took place on a Saturday morning when most of the offices were closed. Any person with a semblance of common sense would seize upon the business opportunity that an influx of people milling around would present.

While they were having dinner with their wives, the topic of Christmas cropped up. How it was celebrated, what it meant, what a business opportunity.

'There you are ladies Christmas is coming, you should start thinking about Christmas in and around the vineyard,' proposed Tom.

The ladies were bewildered, it was the best part of a year away and had only just got over the last one.

'No, no, if you are going to do something business wise for Christmas now's the time to plan and get prepared.'

There were smiles as the penny dropped, the ideas were flowing. They wanted to know if the vineyard shop and restaurant would be ready. 'September' said Tom

The boys smiled; they were all thinking along the same lines. Whatever the women do, it really doesn't matter, it will get them off our backs and give them something to do.

They decided that they had to be different.

'It's basically a vineyard, we can get clothes, electrics, jewelry for Christmas presents anywhere. You could literally hear the minds ticking over. Christmas not only means presents and toys, it means church, family, food, specialty food, good quality food. Food that would be associated with a vineyard, wine, the areas that grew grapes.' The ladies were now on a mission.

Friday rolled round again; the football chat was going along nicely; Jim was chatting to the waitresses.

When she got bored, Jim interrupted the football chat. 'By the way guys I invited Peter to join us this afternoon'.

There was stunned silence, they thought that Jim was having them on.

'Honest, I was at the club and who should come in with Grant Austin but Peter. He saw me straight away we chatted for a bit as he always does. 'Eh Bert, he asked If I had seen you lately. Of course, I couldn't lie could I, so I told him that I would be seeing you this Friday.'

'You really are a prick" muttered Bert still not believing him.

Just then, who should walk in the door but Peter.

'You are a prick,' said Bert 'you did invite him here.'

'Well, he kept asking about you. '

Peter saw the guys and walked over,

Jim got him a chair and introduced him to Tom and Kev. Bert and Peter shook hands as if they were long lost friends, Jim smiled and Bert smiled back, with a look that could kill

Peter had dropped his wife off at a class and thanked Jim for inviting him for a beer while he waited.

'Your buddy Bert is doing the same, his wife's at Wal Mart', trying to get the conversation started

'I had a few drinks with a buddy of yours a few weeks ago' said Jim,

'Who's that' answered Peter.

'Archie the accountant.'

'That arsehole' muttered Peter, 'accountant he couldn't add up to ten'

'Jim got on with him ok" said Bert smirking.

Peter said that he didn't think that Jim knew Archie.

Jim told him the story of their drunken evening.

'He's something, else, isn't he?' Peter said.

'You got to know him then?' asked Kev.

Peter told the story of how he had worked with him for about ten years.

'That must have been fun,' said Bert

'What you have to realize about him is that he is introverted, a bully, shy, abrupt, and no class.'

'Just what Jim was saying, a really pleasant guy. In fact, the only guy I know that likes him is Jim,' said Tom

Peter told everybody that Jim was nuts, but then again, he had spent the best part of ten years working with a guy who was anti-social, insecure, didn't know how to socialize, got drunk easily, out of his depth in the workplace, suffered from total insecurity. He also had an aversion to non-Canadians except those of the nationality of the woman he was hooked up with at the time.'

'I take it you didn't like him,' stated Tom, "what I don't understand is how the hell did you work with him for ten years?'

I could spend the next ten minutes explaining that' said Peter.

'Go ahead', said Jim, 'we are all ears.

If looks could kill, Bert would have slaughtered Jim. He knew Peter of old, once you started him talking you couldn't shut him up.

'Other than him I liked my job,' 'he hadn't got a clue about what we did and what I did so he left me alone. I had ten years to go to retirement so I sat back and went for the ride.

He told everyone that he ran the transport division, but again because of his abrupt and introverted personality staff were leaving and as with a lot of companies run by accountants' business was disappearing. The family that owned the company were loyal to the nth degree, they had had somebody waiting in the wings for some time, someone with some expertise in the business, someone with some class. This person had an offer elsewhere and left. As ever and as always, he was in the right place at the right time. They started this other company and gave him the job of running it.

Of course, with his personality he couldn't get or keep staff and or clients. As he couldn't relate to staff and or clients and was always in a state of flux with his women, he spent his life staring at his computer screen. The nationality, lifestyle and culture of the woman dictated as to what he looked at on the internet.

Mind you it had its perks. We went to lunch together most days as it was charged to the company. The downside was that I had to sit and listen to Archie pontificate on the weather, what the current subject of his internet research was etc. etc. as long as it was related to him. I am the first to admit I hung to his coat tails, simply for the benefits as we milked the company. We would go to conferences and take advantage of the freebies, not that he knew anybody at these functions or made any attempt to get to know anybody.

The only people that Archie got to know were, the reps from the various companies we bought things off. The money spent, though not large in big companies' terms was substantial. Of course, the reps would do anything to get and keep the business, so they sucked up to Archie, took him golfing, on fishing trips, bought him dinners. Even though they didn't like him it was a means to an end. Archie really didn't care about them either he called them pricks and used them to suit himself whenever he could. Really, they deserved each other.

I would go home and laugh about it with my wife. Her favorite question would be, 'so what health program is he on this week'.

To my relief, over the final couple of years boy wonder was under strict instructions from his latest conquest, he went walking at lunch time. There was nothing more that Archie liked than a hearty lunch or big dinner. But times they were a changing. The latest girl friend bought him one of those fancy computerized watches so that she could monitor his activity He would come to me extolling the virtues of this food, why you should only eat what this culture eats. Two years before, he had done the same only read in Russian.

It was funny, he would hardly eat anything when she was around controlling his diet, but get him out of her clutches, at dinners, expensed or treated lunches and he ate like a pig. Out with reps at dinner, he always finished off with port, not that he liked it or new anything about it, but it was the most expensive thing on the menu.

He was chastising me about drinking or eating milk products. His girl friend had told him dairy products were evil. He looked at me and told me how great he was feeling since he gave them up, look how good I look and how much weight I've lost. So, I asked him how long he had been on that particular diet. About a week I just cracked up said Pete, the guys a fruit loop.'

Bert and Tom chuckled and Bert told Peter that he was the second person who had had to go through that inquisition, ask Jim. By the way, what's the truth as to how Archie ended up back in accounting', said Bert

'It's ironic,' said Peter, 'but he got shafted by someone he had hired and trusted. People in the know wondered what he was doing when he hired the weasel as he was known in the business. Here was a guy who had almost bankrupted his previous employer and was fired. He had been unemployed for over a year, nobody would hire him. The weasel worked his magic behind the scenes, Archie, was an amateur, easy picking for the weasel. The weasel's sole intent as it had been at his previous company was to destroy his boss and take over. In this case it wasn't difficult as Archie hadn't got much of a clue regarding the technical side of the business. I didn't know the intricacies, but from what I understand, one morning Archie was escorted out by a couple of male members of the family, never to be seen there again.

As the last member of the group Jim to actually see Archie, how his healthy lifestyle was doing.'

'Judging from our night out, not too well'.

Peter went on to explain that that didn't surprise him as if ever there was a free meal or drinks in the offing, he would be there gorging himself. Peter went on to tell how he had gone on the fishing trip with him. You should have seen him devour the buffet and free wine. The girl friend would have had kittens. Believe it or not when he got back to the office he was lecturing people on the virtues of small portions and healthy living.'

'Did he say whether he was still married Jim, or is he working on number four,' asked Peter

'You know I haven't a clue and I don't really give a shit.'

19.

The condo was rising out of the ground, or to be precise out of the concrete bunker which would be a couple of floors of the underground parking garage. Over the road amidst the construction of the store and restaurant the buds on the vines were sprouting tufts of green.

Downtown the traffic circle to nowhere was nowhere to be seen, it was gone and replaced by conventional roads much to the delight of the citizens. There had been phenomenal interest in the newly created space at much reduced taxes.

The river valley was looking like a building site but the river canal was clearly defined as it worked its way through the city.

The boys were taking a ride round the areas of land that the city had set aside for them as parking lots. One plot in particular, right on the edge of the city, caught Tom's attention. It seemed to roll above the river.

'That's much too pleasant to be a parking lot, we should do something creative with it.'

They got out of the vehicle, walked over the land, picking up the lovely black dirt they were even more convinced that it shouldn't be a parking lot

'More grapes' said Bert.

'No, the vineyard is the center piece of our lifestyle project, we can't develop a similar thing out here,' said Tom. 'What else can we grow'

'What about a garden center?' asked Kev.

'Don't we have enough developments going on, we need to get some of them completed and up and running. All I am saying,' said Tom 'is that this land is much too good to stick tarmac on'

'What about garlic. There is a place in California where all that they grow is garlic. I forget what it's called but it's known as the garlic capital of the US'

'If it is grown in California it probably won't grow here' said Jim

'It will" said Tom, 'I grow it in my back yard'

'The beauty of it is that it doesn't take too much effort'

'Of course, it will,' said Bert. 'All plants take a lot of effort'

Tom explained that you plant it in the fall, cover it with leaves or straw or something like that. Comes the spring you take off the covering and watch the shoots grow. When the scapes start to develop seed heads you pinch the seed heads out. Then you break off the scapes and cook with them or put them in salads or put them in your stir fries. Once the garlic leaves start to go yellowy brown and die off you pick the bulbs which is usually around the middle of July.

'So are you going to come up here and plant the stuff' asked Kev

'I don't think so' said Tom, 'why don't we get some students to do it for us'

I have a far better idea,' said Jim.

'Here we go,' said Bert

'We have all the pieces' said Jim. 'We go to the schools or agricultural college, donate the land, they do the work and then sell the garlic at our vineyard store. Any profit goes to the school. Just as in California it will bring in the consumers, they will buy because it is locally grown; grown by the students with the profits ploughed back to subsidize their education.'

'Jim', said Bert, 'that is brilliant

The venture was set up, the schools thrilled, the newspaper made the most of it with a special supplement. Everywhere you went, the citizens of Mere Folly were talking about it, the boys and the mayor were reveling in it

On the outskirts the rest of the parking lots were being developed Realtors and businesses were loving all the action as not only were people spending money, but the development was creating so much interest that people were looking at moving to Mere Folly

The newspaper was praising the virtues of the development, advertising was pouring in. There were of course the dissenters' writing letters to the editor that for some reason didn't get printed.

This was also an election year in Mere Folly, a couple of years before, the mayor was a bit dubious as to whether he should even stand again. At their table in their cafe the boys were discussing the election, although some six months away they wanted to know what the Mayor had in mind.

The boys were concerned, as replacing him like for like would be next to impossible. If anybody would have said to the boys three or four years ago that they desperately wanted this Mayor to stay in office they would have suggested a visit to a psychiatrist. Their minds were put at ease when the Mayor advised them that he was looking forward to standing again.

'What about the council said Tom".

The Mayor said that he wouldn't shed a tear if a couple of them didn't make it.

'I am sure that can be arranged,' said Bert. There must be a couple of "friends' that you could introduce

The Mayor was making himself at home at the boys table when Bert asked him how his girlfriend was doing, they all wondered how he really got away with it, were the boys the only ones who knew what was going on, it was a certainty his wife didn't.

'Can you really trust her,' asked Bert

'What do you mean.'

Bert opened up and asked the mayor what would happen if they fell out with each other,

"Hell, hath no fury like a woman scorned" quoted Tom.

One thing that the mayor wasn't and that was stupid. He was a bit insular which was proving to be a bonus. 'She, nor my wife for that matter has any idea of the relationship I have with you guys and what we are up to and I want to keep it that way.'

'That's a relief,' said Kev.

The boys had come a long way since first meeting the Mayor and one false move or word could screw everything up. Eventually, the penny had dropped with him, as the boys told him that he couldn't afford to dump her.

Then the boys brought up the fact that she was a fair bit younger than him and what did she see in him. The Mayor was in his early sixties, about six feet tall, a gangling figure with glasses and greying hair, he wore white socks with black shoes, not much in the way of worldly experience. Definitely not the picture one would conjure up if one were describing a gigolo having it off with a much younger woman.

The boys laughed as he kept reminding them that 'the sex is great' not quite understanding how a guy like him had the energy. They were adamant that the sex would either keep him fit or kill him, perhaps it wasn't the sex that was aiming to kill him

The councillor was getting rather frustrated though, not necessarily sexually you see but she wanted a more exciting life. In her position having sex on the mayor's couch was getting rather passé.

Deep down though she dreamt of her next step; being Mayor of Mere Folly. She anguished over the fact that if he stood for re-election in November then it would be another four years before she could run for the bloody job. She made up her mind, she was going to be the next Mayor of Mere Folly. The problem was, there were only six months to devise and conceive a means to get rid of him without creating any perception, inference, gossip or speculation that she was involved in his demise.

She had enough on him to create a storm but whatever she did or said as he departed, he would bring her into it and she would have no chance of winning the election. The councillor could just imagine the local gossip. "Her and him you have to be joking" she couldn't stand that.

How could she do it, how could she hasten his departure. Departure, depart this world, dead, that's it she will have to kill him or get him killed she thought. In that way he wouldn't be able to stop her becoming mayor and who knows what.

Her knickers were getting wet as the more she was thinking of her idea, the more excited and aroused she was getting. Ironically, it reminded her that she was late for her clandestine meeting with himself.

'Boy, you were ready for that my darling,' the Mayor said panting a little.

She smiled as she couldn't stop thinking of how she could do him in as she started to get aroused again, but then she chuckled and shelved it as once in a session was as much as he could offer and any more would probably kill him anyway. It would be great to kill him she thought, a heart attack while they were at it would be perfect. Mmmmmm that would mean a lot of explaining to do, plan B was definitely a better option she thought

The Mayor was getting his trousers ready to put on, still feeling a bit light headed, "let's go for dinner",

'Why do you want to go for dinner,' she said.
'It's called hunger.'

The councillor looked at him; what a sight, a sixty whatever year old in his white underpants, trousers round his ankles, white socks.

'Errrm, I'd love to but I have a couple of things I have to do,' she lied.

Enough is enough she thought as she lay in bed and thought of what she had just had sex with. Ugggh, she shivered, that's as much as I can take, I have to get rid of him. Three o'clock in the morning, flat on her back staring at the ceiling, still trying to figure out how to get rid of him. She had gone over and over it again and again as to why she couldn't just break off the relationship. He's got a split personality, she knew that he would really get bent out of shape, get even and do what he could to destroy her. Even if she didn't break off the relationship and then told him that she was going to stand for election as mayor, he would turn nasty and the relationship would end. It will be difficult enough to win an election, but with him doing what he could to destroy her nearly impossible. Death was the only answer.

Although the downtown was still in a state of erection, the boys agreed that the farmers market should go on. They sat with the city project manager and asked how the parking lots were doing.

'Almost there,' he laughed.

'What's the joke? Asked Kev.

'There wasn't a joke, it's just the fact that nobody knew they were there and that with no parking, downtown or the immediate vicinity it degenerated into utter chaos.'

'Oh shit," said Bert.

'You guys had better get somebody on this' laughed the project manager.

Tom didn't see a problem, he just told the project manager that it wasn't their problem, it was his job.

The project manager laughed again, 'we have a plan in place, everything is ready to be launched. Parking lots, transport, signage, web site, piece for the newspaper.'

'Why the bloody hell hasn't it been launched then' asked Bert

The project manager, as calm as ever. 'Why?'

The farmers market opened the first Saturday in May. It covered a vast area of the downtown streets. Lots of local vegetables and produce for sale, pretty darned good considering that a month ago the average daily temperature around Mere Folly was minus two, the fields were rock hard and covered in ice and snow. The same vegetables and produce could have been bought at any one of the local supermarkets for a lower price. However, the pleasure of being outside in the relative warmth of the early season sunshine is sheer bliss as opposed to plodding through snud with the cold wind biting at your back. The first couple of outdoor markets of the season represent an opportunity to forget the recent winter, there is something to be said for vegetables and produce from a market.

The crowds built, not only giving the stall holders a welcome opportunity to sell their products, gain financially, but also provide a chance for customers to view the newly renovated downtown and of course perception of the river valley.

The only snag was there was nowhere to park. It was like a zoo.

Sunday morning, the boys sat in the project manager's office.

'Stroke of genius,' said Kev, 'If they had launched the parking plan on the first day, it would only have had limited use as most people try to park as close as possible to the event and ignored the parking scheme. But now having seen the traffic chaos around the market the parking and shuttle facility will be welcomed'

And so, it was.

The project manager's plan was working like a charm. The parking lots, bus links and signage were to be introduced ready for the next Saturday. The 'nominal' charge would appear cheap compared to the catastrophe and torment of the opening Saturday

While the boys and the project manager were solving their immediate problem, the mayor was trying to solve his.

It takes two to tango, the killer and the killed but who would be what. Did either of them realize what the other was thinking. Even though he wanted her dead, until that time he still wanted to have sex with her. She wanted him dead and couldn't face sex with him anymore.

It was easy for him; sex went on until she was dead but for her how could she avoid sex with him without him smelling a rat.

Simultaneously they were thinking of various ways to do the deed, poison traceable, shooting traceable too loud, strangulation traceable. She thought of a hit man, traceable, or is it but where do you find one.

What about making it look like suicide. Would have to be ingenious thought the mayor. Then any means to kill her must be ingenious.

The next day, Friday, their usual meeting in the mayor's office. She was brooding and he was looking forward to it. As she walked in they hugged as usual, once she was close to him the urge took over and before long she was virtually naked on his couch while he did his thing.

'Thank goodness you got a couch' she said breathlessly, it sure beats the desk.

'It was a good idea' he panted, thinking that that would be a waste of money as quite soon she wouldn't get a chance to use it.'

The sex was over and done with quite quickly, she tidied herself up re did the makeup. He was still pulling his trousers up.

'What a sight,' she thought.

She told him she had to run and would be in touch. I'm really going to miss our Friday mornings thought the mayor. I could smother her. Then I would have to get the body out of here, that would be great he thought sarcastically.

'There has to be a way,' she thought,
'There must be a way,' he thought.

She was concerned. What if she did kill him, the chances of getting away with it were remote. What was the alternative. Carry on having sex with him until he wasn't able or died. What if he did die on the job. She wasn't going to be Mayor this time around. After all, could she wait four and a half years. Would she be a shoe in for the job? Perhaps the four years would give her the opportunity to make some money without the pressure of being mayor, after all, she knew what the mayor was up to and he couldn't stress her out any more.

The councillor was a relatively attractive forty-two-year-old. Slightly podgy, but some extra exercise and more careful eating would take care of that. She was liking the good things in life that her position was giving her so why not milk the system and expenses as so many of her colleagues and politicians did.

Plan B was formed, it wasn't to get rid of him but to use him as much as possible so that she could take over in four years time. Over the next four years she would ingratiate him, so that he would be her biggest supporter. She enjoyed sex, so why not carry on with him, at least she knew where he had been, he wasn't likely to two time him as she knew he couldn't stand the pace and he never had sex with his wife anymore. Besides that, having what appeared to be a strong marriage helped him to stay in office.

She would start to make sure that he knew not only that she was supporting him in his election campaign but that he could trust her.

It was quasi blackmail in that she wasn't threatening him in a way that he would recognize but efficiently in a cunning, deceitful and manipulative manner

The Mayor popped in to join the boys Friday afternoon for a quick one, he sat down, looked around to survey the café, mainly to see if there was anybody he knew or anybody that could over hear him. He looked at the new waitresses and asked who hired them. "I bet you'd like that job, Jim?'

Jim nodded and smiled biting his lip. Kev chuckled; he knew Jim was itching to tell the Mayor that he actually hired them as he owned the place, but they had learned their lesson, the boys just smiled.

Mario didn't really know the Mayor, but they soon got along as Mario told the mayor that he was going to be opening two more eateries on the banks of the mighty river. Of course, the Mayor who knew nothing about this but was intrigued to learn, as he smarmed all over the guy who thought could do him some good, especially as he owned a bunch of restaurants

Great; thought Tom, this is what we don't want, the mayor learning too much about what was going on.

Bert trod on Mario's foot under the table suggesting that he should shut up. Mario got the message, saw somebody he knew and wandered off to chat

The Mayor was straight in at the boys wanting to know why he wasn't told about Mario and the restaurants.

'It's only just happened' said Tom, 'that's why Mario's here and that's his way of telling us that everything is on side I suppose" lied Tom.

That appeared to shut up the Mayor who was quite happy thinking that he had made a new important friend. In his mind he was chewing over the fact that he would get the scoop from Mario when they were alone together

'Besides,' said Bert, 'I don't know that we should be telling you anything. Who knows what kind of pillow talk is going to be coming out of your mouth when you are in bed with herself''

As another round of beer arrived, the Mayor, to everybody's amazement lowered his head with his eyes staring and in tones that prepared them for a revelation.

'Yes, I've been thinking about that.'

Was it the beer talking or was he in earnest? Had the mayor seen religion, was he taking the piss or coming clean as he told them that he was concerned about what the councillor knew about him and had on him.

Bert told him that he could be in for an unpleasant surprise if he upset her.

'What would happen if she found a young stud and turfed you, or perhaps worse, your wife found out,' emphasized Kev

All of a sudden, they were all talking in hushed tones. The mayor seemed relieved to be able to open up. After all his only "friend' that he could talk to was the councillor, he admitted how stupid he was.

Then he really opened up, "I even thought of getting rid of her"

"Well," said Kev "That would be good she would find somebody else".

'No, you don't get it, I thought with what she knew, I couldn't trust her. Get rid of her. Kill her"

Tom knocked his beer over.

'That's a waste,' said Jim.

'Sod me' said Bert,

'I meant the beer, not her,' said Jim

The Mayor went on to say that he had been worried sick about what she could do to him and felt that getting rid of her was the only option.

'Hold on', Tom was excited as he gathered his thoughts.

'Don't forget there are two of you' and went on to explain that if they parted, he could also damage her credibility,

'I'm sure that one thing that she really wants is your job, if word got out about your relationship you two would be up what's-its creek without a paddle, neither of you would be Mayor.'

The sense of panic calmed down, after much discussion the Mayor thought and understood that it would be better if he stayed with her.

'You still like the sex, don't you,' said Bert.

'Well, yes.'

'Well carry on enjoying it and the sex.'

As he was being tutored, they explained to him that things were going to be very very different. They then told him in no uncertain terms, "you don't trust her, you don't confide in her, you watch her like a hawk, you use her more than you use her at the moment and you only tell her what you want her to hear.'

He felt a whole load of darkness, doubt and misery lifted the way ahead seemed bathed in sunshine.

Later, the leading question was mooted, "do you honestly think he would have done it". One thing that they were convinced of was that their affinity with the Mayor was a little stronger, but they still didn't know where the councillor fitted in.

Tom laid back in his chair, 'funny thing politics, the "silly servants" do the work while the politicians play around, that's why there is so much sex and scandal hidden away in the ivory towers.'

Then they got on to the grossly overweight health minister and what a great advert for health with heis triple chin, he's put on extra weight since he's been in that position. The free dinners and entertaining must agree with him.

You would think by now that those who did make it to their lofty positions would grow up and stay away from the scandal and social media comments. They all use social media on a regular basis, most of the time to good effect, however you have to laugh when every now and again one of them destroys theirs's or somebody's reputation by pressing that button too soon

The boys were amongst the many who couldn't stand the government, be it city, provincial or worse still federal. They thought that they were a bunch of inexperienced prima donnas. Comments regarding the government flowed. They thought that they had it bad with what they had ruling the province but what about those poor sods in BC. Their political parties are all so busy being holier than thou with respect to the environment and being politically correct that they will never stay in power long enough to achieve anything. It's supposed to be such an environmentally proper province yet they still dump their effluent into the ocean, welcome to the real world. They also forget that they will need money to save the planet and the peasants will really revolt when they can't afford to live. As one of the guys said, look at the price of housing there and wait until the price of gas goes through the roof perhaps then the penny will drop and common sense will prevail.

'I doubt it,' the boys agreed in unity.

Headlines on the front page of the Mere Folly newspaper proclaimed that despite all the construction going on property taxes were being cut by twenty percent.

Communication to the editor poured in; from "it's an election stunt" to "where's the money coming from" to "they'll bankrupt the city".

"Makes you wonder what the rhetoric would be if they had some bad news," laughed Bert. They were having their weekly meeting at the newspaper and decided to fight fire with fire.

They told the Mayor that he was going to be interviewed by the newspaper's senior journalist.

'We've only got one journalist.' said Henry "

'Well then he's senior, then, isn't he?' responded Kev.

The Mayor was told to write an interview question and answer piece. He squirmed at the thought. Especially when he was told he had three days.

'Listen, if you handle this properly it will give you a leg up for your election campaign. You were a school teacher it should be a piece of cake for you. Just like writing an essay. Mind you if you don't do it you'll be dead in the water - your choice'.

A week later the Mayor's interview was published.

From the new businesses along the river, the new library being built, the vineyard, the revitalization of the downtown, the removal of the traffic circle to nowhere, the twinning of the bypass. The restaurants and businesses were lining up to get a spot in Mere

Folly. Citizens are going to be subsidized by businesses who are more than happy to pay taxes to be part of the city trading environment. Income is going to increase hugely from tax income on the existing non-retail businesses downtown, obviously they won't be able to afford these exorbitant taxes and will of course gradually move out being replaced by even more retail, restaurants and specialty entities. The non-retail businesses are already subsidizing the city tax payers from their new locations in the new business parks surrounding the city.

City employees to pay for parking. Why shouldn't they?

Skating on the river will be free

The main road through the city will be a toll road, that is except for residents, this will force through traffic to use the bypass.

If the boys thought that the communications to the editor poured in a couple of weeks ago, all hell broke loose after the mayor's diatribe, but to the amazement of the mayor most of it was positive. Of course, there are cranks everywhere, but they make life so very interesting.

20.

With their respective minds settled on their relationship it didn't take either of them too long to get their lives back to normal. Gone were the days of getting together for a bit of sex and the moron being the mayor's puppet.

There was no way that they trusted each other, but what they did realize was that they needed to remain together to make sure that they knew what was going on. They had their own agendas but still had to know what each other was up to.

So, what better place to stay in touch than in bed doing their thing together. It was their first session since getting together again, lying there, getting her breath back, staring at the ceiling, the moron suddenly started complaining about her next-door neighbor having her garden sprinkler on and wasting water.

The mayor nearly fell out of bed, as he wondered, what the dumb bat was talking about now, what's that got to do with me'.

'What a shame,'

'What a shame, is that all you can say,' as the bell went off in her head

She sat stark upright in the bed, the mayor ogling her breasts, 'What if I start by enforcing people to cut back on their water consumption, I'll be the green queen',

'That should be worth a few votes. Why would you want to stop people using water, they pay for it' said the mayor as he lay there, eyes still transfixed on her breasts

Why asked the mayor

She'd read about water preservation in articles and heard people talk about it on TV, but really didn't understand enough about it to answer the mayor's question. She was racking her brain to think up an answer and was getting frustrated doing so.

'Look, dickhead," she suddenly paused. She had never lost her temper with him before or called him a name. She waited for his angry response;

There wasn't one, he said nothing. She didn't know it but that was how his wife treated him, he was used to it.

'Not only could we cut out all those water wasters we could make a tidy income from water meters' she thought aloud

'Water meters'

'Yes, we could tell all home owners that we were going to install water meters to monitor water usage and provide more accurate bills.'

'Isn't that going to cost a fair bit just to keep tabs on water usage, so that you can seek revenge on your neighbor'

'You really are a dickhead' she reminded him

'Where did you get all this environmental gobbledy gook from all of a sudden.'

'Well, do you remember a couple of weeks ago you chickened out of a meeting with some company that said the city ought to re-evaluate its water meters'

'Not really'

'Well I went and met them, it set my mind thinking'

'About what'

'Every home will have a new water meter installed to accurately monitor water usage.'

'That will be popular, it will cost a fortune' admitted the mayor

'Why buy real ones, think about it, we can launch a water conservation program.'

Over the years she had learnt quickly, now the tables were turning

'We don't have to install meters that actually work'

He smiled.

'Because they have the security tag on them nobody interferes with them or really gives them a second glance'

'So how are you going to gather the information if these meters are just useless bits of plastic.'

'Simple, we will leave the existing ones there and keep using them.'

'But what about the additional information and data?'

'Easy, we use what data we collect and invent the other stuff'

'Brilliant,' said the mayor

Moron was still sat there, upright, in the nude, thinking that she was brilliant and ready to take over. She still needed him for the time being, but in four years time she would be Mayor

Of course, we will have to put together a company to operate this scheme and keep our names out of it as much as possible.' The Mayor had learnt a little bit from working with the boys.

'How do you propose that' she said as she got off the bed with a blanket draped over her. Deep down the fact that she wanted to be the top dog was gnawing away at her she wasn't going to be his lap dog any more.

He thought, as he sat on the edge of the bed in his underpants and white socks, of chatting it over with the boys. One thing about the Mayor was that, just like his relationship with the moron, he liked to keep things close to his chest. Gave him that certain feeling of power. No, the last thing he wanted to do was to introduce her to the boys. Deep down the mayor sighed.

What a shithead, she is, great at sex but no brain. That's one thing he learnt with the boys, you can't be good at everything, therefore bring in the expertise.

She was in the bathroom and he was dressing, which gave him some time to slow his thought process down. Actually, it's a blessing, the last thing he wanted to do was to confide in her and tell her what was going on.

'What are you thinking about now' she snarled as she came out of the bathroom.

'How we start working on your idea' he lied. What he was really thinking of was that he had to keep sucking up to her. The longer the lead, the less chance he had of controlling her and that wouldn't do.

'I reckon it's a great idea and money maker for us. Do you have a friendly lawyer who would set up the company and keep his mouth shut?'

'What do we need to go through that stuff for?

After all these years together, she's learnt nothing. She's still dumber than dumb, he muttered, she can't be serious.

Previously he would have called her a dumb broad, but under his new regime he slowly remarked, 'it would be better if we did it properly as if it's discovered what we are doing there will be real issues'.

'Are you going to do this or not' as the stimulus of power started to cloud her mind.

His mind was racing, he could see working with her on a scam such as this would be a disaster, yet if he played his cards right he could set her up and get rid of her.

'Why don't you set the company up, then go to the bank and get an account organized.'

Knowing full well what he was doing he asked her the rhetorical question which was, whether she wanted him to be president. Obviously, this was the last thing he wanted; in fact he wanted no part of the scam.

'No, I will be president' she said defiantly. 'You can be the consultant'

'I tell you what my darling, you have it as your baby, if you want my help I will be there for you'. He presumed that there would be no fightback. There wasn't

Great, thought the Mayor, what a pleasure to be working with an idiot

The Mayor popped in to have a beer with the boys. The more he thought about the moron's idea, the more he felt it was the perfect way to set her up.

Should he mention this to the boys?

He decided to wait and see how the conversation went. Going through his head was the fact of telling them and asking their advice, it could cement and even concrete his relationship with them.

The Mayor was the first to arrive, however the table was taken. It's Friday, the Mayor said to the guy at the door, yes, the guy new that and looked puzzled.

'Aren't the boys coming?

'The boys' inquired the waiter, maître de or whatever he was. 'Yes, the boys'

'You're new here?', as the penny dropped

'All of three days' he smiled

'Then nobody told you that that table over there is reserved from 3 onwards every Friday'.

Then horror, he saw who was at the table, the moron, a couple of female councillors and another lady he didn't recognize. 'Is nothing sacred' he muttered and dived out

Crossing the road was Tom and coming around the corner were Kev and Jim.

'What are you, the welcoming committee'

The Mayor ushered them up the street away from the restaurant windows.

'What's going on' said Bert getting out of his car

'Our table's been taken'

'No big deal' said Bert, 'We'll get it back'

'You don't understand' the Mayor laughed. 'It's who has taken our table; the moron and a couple of councillors'

'Well, they have a right to go to any eatery they choose,' said Tom

'Yes, but I can't go in there and sit with you guys'

'But they don't know us from a hole in the ground and we are happy about that'

'Don't you see, I would have to introduce you and that could lead to questions and talk, get my point'

'Tell you what we will go in and report back'

The boys turned their backs and walked back to Chat, the mayor stood there, shell shocked. Convinced that everybody had deserted him. Gone was the chance to confide in them, which he decided was to their detriment not his

They walked into Chat. It was fairly busy. The women were still at their table.

The new waiter greeted them. 'Table for four gentlemen'

'Our table is taken' Tom said so that the new waiter could hear.

Who hired him, Bert said looking directly at Jim. Couldn't have been you could it, it's a guy.

Just then, Bridget, one of the regular waitresses came over, 'I'll take over"
What happened to our table. 'Long story,' said Bridget

'Try us' said an impatient Jim and by the way, who hired him.

'Another long story, but Mario was in.'
'Say no more,' said Tom, 'we'll deal with him.'

'I'm so sorry, but they came in, walked over to the table and said that they would take it. I told them that it was already reserved. They said yes it was; for them. What could I do. Would you like me to ask them to move?' 'I would enjoy that. All afternoon they have been the nastiest pieces of work that I have ever tended to. They treat the staff as if they are pieces of garbage. So, can I get rid of them?'

'No', said Bert, 'Put us at the big table at the back. Bridget, be calm, be patient, everything comes to him or her that waits.'

They were sat at the big oval table at the back of the restaurant. No windows an alcove of brick walls, but from there, each of the boys could see the whole room. Maybe we should have this as our usual table.

'No, I prefer daylight round me, said Kev.

'We'd prefer that as well,' said Jim, 'we like to see what you are up to.'

As Bridget brought the beer Tom asked Bridget to reserve the oval table for them for the next few weeks.

'Hopefully the bitches won't be here next week,' she said, 'then you can have your table back.'

'I am hoping that they are back next week,' said Tom

The others looked at him as if he was nuts.

'Think about it.' Tom broke in, 'There's four women, what would they be doing round a table, think about it; gossiping'

Kev's eyes lit up, 'I am with you, was it not the late great Charley's cousin who dabbled a bit in extra curricula spying,' his mind was working overtime.

'A thing of beauty' said Jim 'Tell me more'

Bert was soon in touch with Charley's cousin who in turn was only too eager to fit something up for them.

They told him that they wanted the same sort of listening device that the cops had planted under the same table.

'I should have left it there'

'You should have done, it would have been far cheaper' said Bert

They had felt a bit sorry for the Mayor, so suggested he pop in to the cafe early in the morning as they wanted to chat with him.

So, while Jim and Tom sat at the regular table the Mayor, Bert and Kev sat at the back testing the reception

'This is great' said the Mayor 'but you can't eaves drop on everybody in here'

They told the mayor about the women taking over the table and their rudeness to the staff. Hopefully they come back on Friday and keep coming back on Fridays.

They suggested to Bridget that the regular table should still be reserved but for the bitches as Bridget liked to call them

Tom and Jim were at the regular table doing the sound test

'I wonder if those pricks down the other end can hear us.' Bert at the other end of the restaurant stuck his finger in the air

'You know the good thing about this' said Tom 'is that they can hear us but we can't hear them, it's about time we were able to talk and say what we want without getting interrupted'

A set of two finger salutes were raised from the far table

Albert came up and whispered, 'can you hear me', then still a whisper but a bit louder, the thumbs went up down the other end. The boys were thrilled, as they sat with a wireless ear piece in their ears.

'I bet after all this they don't turn up now 'said Kev

'Bridget,' called Bert, 'do me a favor, here's my cell number if they come in any other time text me.'

'Sure, but why do you want to know if they come in'

'Just to make sure that you don't throw them out,' said Jim

Bridget blew Jim a kiss and shuffled off

The Mayor was over the moon that the boys had confided in him, once again he felt part of the fraternity. He couldn't hold himself back and poured out his story of the recent happenings with the moron.

Wow said Kev, she's not that stupid is she.

'You bet,' said the Mayor

'We just need to get you re-elected' said Tom 'the next four years are going to be a bit hectic in more ways than one, but at least it will be rather amusing especially if we play our cards right and especially with you having her by the whatsits if she starts to do anything stupid'

The boys rolled up to Chat about 2 pm on the Friday and sat in wait at the large dark table at the back of the cafe. In front of them was a little black box with a green light plugged into a wall outlet. Jim wandered up to the regular table appeared to look out the window and in a quiet voice, 'testing, can you hear me'.

Bert stuck his thumb in the air.

They sat with their beers, earplugs in and waited.

'So, this is the new table now is it' smirked Bridget. 'They are real bitches; you should have let me turf them out the door'

'Patience is a virtue' said Tom, 'besides its quieter down here'

'I wish I knew what you old fools were up to'
'I don't know who I don't trust more you or them'
'Aaah old yes but not so much of the fools' smiled Bert, 'You don't trust us or them but you like us'

She turned and left shaking her head

About half an hour later, there was a sense of relief. The moron and one of the councillors walked in, ignored the waiter at the door and went straight to "their" table. The look of disgust on the staff's faces could be seen from where the boys were sitting. For once they didn't care, they had their afternoon's entertainment mapped out.

'Mmmm Prosecco' said Bert as the women ordered' 'now I understand what the staff go through when you have pricks like that to serve. No thank you's or pleases'.

'There's a chink in the armour' whispered Kev.

'They can't hear you' whispered Jim mockingly.

Laughing, Kev went on, 'it's strange, I don't know whether I will get used to this, I keep waiting for them to respond as I say something, but there they are, only been together for a couple of minutes and are criticizing the other councillor'.

'I suppose that if the tables were turned the missing councillor would be criticizing them'

There had been an agreement to stick together on some minor point but Gretchen decided to question Moron's point. The Moron didn't like that, she wanted them to know who was boss. Then there was an abrupt silence as the other two arrived.

The boys laughed as they could not only see but hear them hugging and loving each other

'All friends again' whispered Tom

'Only until one or two of them aren't there and then I bet the shit hits the fan,' laughed Bert.

The boys yawned their way through most of the afternoon as the women berated other members of council and discussed how bad city hall was run. They were sucking up to the Moron trying to persuade her to stand for Mayor in the November election. She said that she hadn't made up her mind and had an idea that might take a couple of years to implement and leave a legacy. This would lead her into standing in four years time, when with her friends, smile, smile, smile they will take over the City.

Gloria, another ex-realtor, was coming to the end of her first term of office. Another elected official who stumbled into office by saying most of the right things, even though she didn't know what they meant. She had been an instant hit with the Moron as from day one she told her what a pleasure it was working with her. They enjoyed the odd drink or four which helped them get to know each other better

'So, what is this great plan you have for us' Gloria asked.

The boys gulped their beer, the boys were on tenterhooks

The Moron explained that it was all to do with the environment. Then she went on to slate her next-door neighbor,

'I can't stand them, mind you the people on the other side are just as bad'

'You poor thing said Gloria having two lousy neighbors'

The boys were wetting themselves and called for more beer. Jim had to go to the washroom, 'Put them on pause,' he said, 'in case I miss something.'

Bethany the other councillor, again serving her first term on a hiatus after her first year at university doing arts. She was probably elected as the populace thought that they should have a bit of green on the council in more ways than one. The Moron had taken her under her wing and during that time she had gained a liking for Prosecco

'Can you imagine during that hot spell, they actually had sprinklers going on their garden'

'No' exclaimed Bethany

Again, the boys cracked up.

'This is better than watching Manchester United lose said Kev

The Moron went on to explain that she wanted to have stricter water usage by laws enacted and them new water meters fitted to each residence in the City so that they could penalize the water wasters as she called them

'What a great idea' said Bethany

'It will get my vote' added Gloria as another bottle of Prosecco arrived

'It will get my vote as well, 'whispered the Mayor to himself, as he could feel the noose tightening round her neck. He had nipped in through the back door and was listening in in the back office.

Round the oval table the question was of where she was going to get 30,000 mock water meters from was raised. 'I wish we could help her,' said Tom. 'We could even buy them for her if we could find a supplier'

21.

'Thought you guys would be here' said Albert as he sat down at the oval table with the boys.

'Have some lunch' said Tom passing a plate to him as they helped themselves to the family style plates of food

Albert asked how the bug was working

'Perfect'

'Are you getting some juicy stuff'

'Not a lot' said Bert 'but we are getting a lot of entertainment'

'Wish we could find a water meter though,' said Jim as a kind of after thought

'Water meter'

'Yes an imitation water meter'

'What, one on the outside of a house' said Albert 'what do you want one of those for'

'Can't really tell you but we need about thirty thousand of them.'

'Mamma Mia.'

'Mamma Mia I think I can help

'Ok' said Tom, 'So you happen to make those as well.'

'No, I don't but my cousin George does,'

Not another cousin, is there anybody that you are not related to?'

The boys sat spellbound as Albert told them the story on cousin George.

'Cousin George has a little plastic injection molding company, some years ago he did a job for the City, making these water meters. As you know the big expense is setting the mould and everything up in the first place. George set everything up, made some samples, quoted and thought he had at long last got a big account. The City had other ideas. They sent his sample to China who reverse engineered it, chopped his price and the City shafted him.'

'The bastards' said Kev, 'Did he sue them

'He hadn't got the money and anyway what chance does the little guy have and besides that it had nearly bankrupted him putting the prototype together in the first place.'

'How long ago was this' asked Kev

'About eight or nine years, why?'

'Just a thought, we can't blame the present Mayor, he wasn't in charge'

'No, George will tell you the full story but rumor has it that it was a staff engineer who handled it. About a year later, this engineer bought a pretty nice place in Mexico, with the backhander from the Chinese. Let's face it these mayors and councillors are amateurs, haven't got a clue what goes on behind the scenes, they couldn't run a piss up in a brewery"

'Don't we know it' said Tom

'So, cousin George survived?'

'He did, doing quite well, not as good as he could have been though.'

'What does he do now?'

'He makes residential water meters'

The boys broke up into laughter

'For Who'

'He makes knock offs for the black market. They look exactly like the originals because it was his initial mold, including the little sealed tag'

'Yeah, but the reader of the meter will pick up on it'

'That's why he's such a clever little shit. There's a way to pull it off the wall and change the counter. So as long as you remember to change the counter by a few digits every month, you pay next to nothing for water.'

Obviously, he's still in business'

'So far'

'I'm loving this guy' Bert drooled, 'when can we meet him and have we got a deal for him that will enable him to retire and put his feet up,'

Albert was on the phone to George; George was having lunch with the boys and Albert the next day. Just prior to Albert and George turning up, Kev suggested they make sure that Albert was cut in so that he had an investment and there would be less chance of him talking

George sat there with his beer and the family style food as Bert explained what they wanted.

'You want thirty thousand, who for?'

Tom went on to explain that they couldn't tell him but what they did want was a shell with the little sealed tag, to stick on a wall.

'Well, how's that going to work?'

'Ok, seeing as you were shafted by the City, here's the chance for revenge'

Tom explained that the meters would be stuck on the walls of residences, with the residence owner under the impression that they are to monitor the residence's water use. However, no monitoring will be done, the City will literally charge what they feel like.

'So how are you going to gather the information if these meters are just useless bits of plastic.'

'Simple, we will leave the existing ones there, put the new box next to it or below it and keep using them.'

'But what about the additional information and data'

'Easy, they use what data is collected and invent the other stuff'

'That is unbelievable and illegal,' said George

'Yes, but all you are doing is manufacturing the case and we are supplying them. What the person at the City does with them is up to them'

'What do you think?' Kev asked

All went quiet, 'how much?' said George

'We will get as much as we can,' Kev jumped in, 'you don't think that we are going to leave any money on the table for these pricks do you.'

George and Albert were happy with their end of the deal.

'One thing I don't get said George is that your cut is not that much considering it has to go four ways'

Tom looked George in the face, 'That's why we want to do business with you George. Like us you have been shafted, your brains picked and your expertise used to make money for others. We can't do this without each other. As seniors a lot of people treat us with contempt and forget that it was people like us that built the country, the world if you like. Then they turn their backs on us. We are not waiting for God. God will come and claim us when he wants us, until then we are going to be awfully successful, what have we got to lose? No longer are we going to help others make money on our behalf. We have a number of projects on the go.'

'Remember George, 10% of something is better than 100% of nothing'

We will arrange for you to meet with our lawyer and accountant, the deal will be put together properly. We will all be able to sleep at night

They toasted with beer and wine long into the afternoon and then struggled into a taxi

The following week boys sat and listened to Bridget's bitches as she now called them.

'Don't worry' said Jim 'think of the big tips you are getting from them.'

'Don't even go there' she said. 'Evidently last week they didn't even leave one. Nobody wants that table'

'I am going to start work on the water meter project,' said the Moron.

'How much will it be'

'Don't know as yet but its going to be pricey but worth it'

'Think of the water we will save.'

'At least she's still on side,' said Bert

The education department superintendent, Freda, was Gloria's step sister. Different as chalk and cheese. Their father divorced both their mothers.

Dressed in her green business suit she liked to explain to people that she wasn't a teacher, she was the one that they reported to. She was the person responsible for making the schools tick. Divorced for over five years, her husband and her kids had nothing to do with her. In fact, they couldn't stand her. As the kids grew up, she treated them with contempt, just like the iron clad school discipline of the late 19th century, in fact close on abuse until one day her husband had had enough. He literally threw her out. She was despised by the teachers; in fact they called her Freda the fart. Or sometimes tart. She told the others that they were too weak and should make sure that the project happened

'She's queen bitch isn't she' said Jim. I had to check the date, I thought that it was St Paddy's day when I saw her in that green costume.

Why don't you stand for council in November, said the Moron? The four of us could really run the City

'You've got to be kidding, how much do you earn as a councillor?' asked an arrogant Freda

'What does that matter?' the naïve idealist Bethany asked

'I'm not going to work for what you get'

'Well, what do you get?' demanded Gloria.

'Just over 400' said the three glasses of Prosecco

'$400,000' gasped the Moron

It was echoed by the boys in their alcove.

'You mean teachers can't get pay rises and these glorified paper pushers are getting that. Somethings wrong in fffin paradise' croaked Bert

The boys could sense though that even though these women were having a drink together there was no love lost between them especially after the superintendent's drunken statement.

That comment by Freda, abruptly brought the evening to a close, as there was silence in the ear plugs. The three councillors got up virtually in unison and walked for the door, leaving Freda sat there

Bridget was near the table and smiled as she asked Freda if she should bring her the tab.

A few minutes later, Bridget came by the oval table.

'The bitch never even left a tip.'

'I do hope that they come next week' said Bert, 'but somehow I don't think that the superintendent will make it.'

Kev was on the phone to the Mayor, telling him that he should pop down to Chat as his friends had left. Within fifteen minutes, the Mayor was walking through the restaurant door. Literally, just as he sat down at the oval table, his phone rang.

'Yes, my darling', he smiled at the boys who were laughing, 'I know that you need me, I will be round in about half an hour, of course I care'

'Surprise, surprise' said Tom as he briefed the mayor as to what had gone on. Then they explained to the mayor that they could provide the water meters and told him to go and console his girl-friend and make her happy by telling her that a friend can get hold of the 30,000 water meters, 50% down and 50% upon delivery. We will tell you exactly how much later'

'You are joking of course'

Bert, poker faced, 'Mr. Mayor, as you get to know us, you will learn that one thing we never joke about is money, now clear off shag her, tell her about the meters and to start putting the cash together'

Somewhat shell shocked, he dived for the door, the boys themselves were breathing rather heavily

'What a day,' said Tom.

'I'm shattered just thinking about the Mayor' said Kev, 'Imagine having to go off now and satisfy your wife or girl friend'

'It makes your eyes water,' said Tom

'Oh no' said Bert, 'Look who's walked in, Mrs. Mayor'

'Bridget', shouted Kev, he then whispered 'put those three ladies at our table'

'We had better protect our investment' said Kev as he texted a message to the Mayor warning him that his wife had turned up at Chat so if he was going to use that as an alibi forget it, he signed off 'hope the sex was good, you owe me yet again, love Kev'

They put the ear plugs in, the saga continued Mrs. Mayor was holding court.

'My husband, the Mayor, does come in here from time to time to meet with important people, I don't see him here though of course he is probably wining and dining with other important people'

Again, this was proving great entertainment at the oval table.

Then they found out that he had plans to stand as the leader of the Provincial Liberal Party.

'We have to have words, with this clown as that could put a lot of our ideas in jeopardy,' said Tom

'Worse still, the Moron could be the Mayor comes November' added Jim

The Mayor wasn't too concerned at what was going over at Chat, he was lying on his back looking at the ceiling with the Moron cuddled up to him head on his chest. She was telling him the story of Gloria's step sister, a woman they thought was a friend.

'Do you know how much she earns, $400,000. Yes $400,000 and she's such a tight arse. How can they pay people like that that much money? Its despicable. Well, she won't be in our group any more, Gloria doesn't like her step sister much anyway. $400,000.

'Terrible, terrible,' said the mayor The mayor continued his plan of sucking up to her, he was sure that that it will be reviewed if the appropriate people were informed. He suggested that she should talk to Gloria and Bethany about letting their friends know when she asked how he thought what should be done.

He was waiting to seize his opportunity, then he dropped it on her.

'By the way I have found a supplier for your water meters'

She was all over him, kissing him, with her hands all over his body. He was enjoying that.

'A contact' he said as she kissed him again.

'Alright' her hands all over him, 'tell me more'.

The mayor explained that this guy will produce exact replicas with the metal security tags, but he wants 50% up front.

'How much my darling' as she nibbled his ear which sent a jolt through him

'Oooh' he said rolling over on top of her

'Later' she said, 'How much'

'$100 each'

'That's $3 million'

Here we go, thought the Mayor this is when the shit hits the fan and she explodes

'If that's what it takes, I'll show that dumb school whatever she is who makes money'

'Let's go for it and the meters'

A little while later and it was a little while, 'It's up to you' said the mayor, 'Start getting it organized so that you can pay the deposit and get things moving'

The Mayor told her he would stay out of it, it was her baby. At council he would cast his vote for the project if needed. He was pretty confident that it would go through council so to protect himself he told her that he would vote against her.

'Why would you do that' she moaned.

'Think about it, people couldn't say that we were in cahoots could they and then it makes it easier for us both if I can sneak in when you need me'

She smiled

He smiled back, knowing that he wasn't incriminated, and as the boys would say, he had her by the whatsits.

The following morning, the mayor had only been in his office a couple of minutes, when in walked the engineer responsible for the City's water management.

In varying capacities, the engineer had been in his position for over twenty years. Although he reported to the mayor and council, he felt that they were just a minor irritant and something of an inconvenience that he had to put up with as he ran his department.

He was rather pompous, despised by his staff and difficult to work with as a number of councillors had determined over the years

'Some time ago,' his words, he had been approached by a representative from a water meter manufacturing an installation company. He suggested that the City should start a water meter replacement scheme. The existing meters are ancient and subject to breakdown he advised the director. They could provide the opportunity to easily monitor water usage, real time leak alerts, high usage notifications, and allow the City to perform meter reading quickly and easily. These new meters would help the City reduce water consumption. The work would take about an hour to complete on each residence. They would install a transmitter on each residence allowing the City to read the water meter from outside a residence thus eliminating the need for the meter reader to gain access to a property to read the meter. The engineer said that had given the aging meters a great deal of thought over the past couple years. After numerous discussions with the water meter replacement company, he was now satisfied that replacement was the way to go. He was now ready to authorize and push on with the scheme so he thought that the time was right to update the mayor.

'So how much is this scheme of yours going to cost,' said the mayor

'About ten to twelve million'

The mayor gulped. 'You what'

'Mr. Mayor you can't let the infrastructure and utilities of the City gradually deteriorate.'

'The only benefit to the resident is that high water usage can be quickly detected ', said the mayor and this may or may not suggest a leak.'

'Who is this company, can I see your due diligence on it'

This really pissed off the engineer.

'I'm telling you this is a quality company and the meters are safe.'

The engineer was getting out of his chair as the Mayor lost it with him'

'What are you up to trying to ram this scheme down my throat. I'm amazed how you have all the plans in place and are now telling me. When were you planning to start this scheme?'

The engineer made for the door and on is way out, turned and looked back

'By the way,' added the engineer in his smug way, 'if this doesn't go through, there could be some revelations that are disclosed about some of the projects you have been involved in.'

The engineer was gone, the mayor was stunned.

The mayor was in touch with the boys, he sounded somewhat agitated, 'We have to chat somewhere really private'

At one of the Boys' houses, later in the afternoon the Mayor rolled up, it didn't take a rocket scientist to figure out that he was flustered.

'What's up with you has she dumped you'

Ignoring the jibe, the Mayor explained that he hadn't been in his office two minutes when the water engineer came to see him and proceeded to tell them the story of the visit.

'One minute the water meters are falling apart and the next there are two schemes in place to replace them'

The Boys laughed, 'That's going to really help her ladyship's plan isn't it. '

'Hold on,' said the mayor.

'This isn't funny, you are missing the point'.

'Oh, the engineer threatening you.'

'Suppose he does have something on me'

'Some of the things you've been up to he probably has'

'What if he has' said the Mayor

'Well wouldn't it be useful to ask him what he has got on you'

'You bastards are heartless; something probably did slip through the cracks over the years. I don't want to take the chance'

'Have you got anything on him?'

Other than he has been at the City about twenty years and nobody likes him, no!'

Something was going around in Tom's head. He asked the mayor if he remembered a program to replace the meters about eight or ten years ago.

'I wasn't mayor then and it wasn't until I became mayor that I started to take a closer look at what was going on.'

'Did you ever' the boys chuckled

'I'm wondering if your friend the engineer is the same guy that shafted George' asked Tom

The boys were convinced, it had to be him, but they needed proof.

Kev took out his phone. 'George, its Kev. Quick question. I know it was ten years ago, can you remember the name of the City engineer who shafted you and can you remember what he looked like'

'Arthur Conroy, how could I forget. Great George, see you soon'

'That's him' said the Mayor, 'the bastard'

Kev explained how George said that he would recognize him anywhere. In fact, the odd time he has been in City Hall he had seen him.

Then the most difficult bit, how could they prove that he actually got a back hander from the company to implement their scheme. They were convinced that there was no way after such a long time that they could find any evidence of money changing hands.

The Mayor said that he could get the documents to do with the deal together from the archives so that they could review and see if they could glean something.

There was something that stuck in their craw and kept niggling away at them. Then the penny dropped. These water meters that were installed some eight or nine years ago, was it a similar scheme that the Moron was plotting.

'Hold on, who manages this water billing enchilada,' said Kev. 'Don't tell me, Conroy'

'Right first time' jumped in the Mayor

'I have an idea,' said Tom

The Mayor followed the boys through the garage and outside while Tom grabbed a screw driver and some pliers.

'Let's take a look at that meter' said Tom forcing his screw driver between the meter and the wall, popping it off.

It fell on the floor.

'There's nothing there' exclaimed Jim. It's just a bloody box'

They went next door to Bert's house. Same thing as the box fell on the floor. They laughed as there were no mechanical bits or wires to be seen.

'The Moron would love this' said Bert

'I think it's time to visit Mr. Conroy,' said Kev

However, they decided that discretion was the better part of valor and that they should plot and scheme a plan of action so that they could find out what was happening and what the utilities department was up to.

The Boys decided that the last thing that they should do would be to storm the department and take prisoners. They felt that the Mayor should take control, in this way Mr. Conroy couldn't bully or go after him

'Why not brief the moron and you and her wait until Mr. Conroy is away and pop in under the pretense of getting an understanding of how the utilities area works.'

The Mayor briefed the Moron on what he had discovered. She thought to herself that it was good to have him on her side, for the time being anyway

They drove over to the building where the utilities were administered. The receptionist told them that Mr. Conroy works on an appointment only basis and was in a meeting. The Mayor suggested that Mr. Conroy would see him without an appointment and besides that as the Mayor he didn't need her permission to visit any of the City's facilities.

Just then a bespectacled young man came through the main door. 'Mr. Mayor, to what do we owe this honor' the mayor was thrilled at being addressed like that and liked the young man straight away.

The Mayor introduced the Moron and the purpose of their visit,

'It's a shame you came today as Mr. Conroy is never in on a Monday or Tuesday'.

'Oh no, Mr. Conroy told me to pop in any time. He said he would show me around and buy lunch

The Mayor and the moron smiled at each other not believing their luck.

'Is that every Monday and Tuesday he is away' enquired the Mayor. 'Yes, said Rodney, he told me that when I have fifteen years' service at a senior managerial position then I only need to work three days as long as I remain in touch with the office'

'Should I contact Mr. Conroy to let him know of your visit.'

'No need Rodney, I am sure he works hard and deserves his time off, what if you show us round'

Feeling very important, Rodney showed the mayor and the Moron the computer room and explained how the data from the meters came in and was transferred to the billing room.

'So, take my house, where does my water use data come in' asked the Mayor

Rodney took the mayor's address and keyed it into a computer. On the screen was a graph showing his month-by-month water consumption.

'How does that compare with last year'

Rodney pulled up last year's graph

'Funny that' said the Moron, 'exactly the same as last year, can you print me off the last four years'

'No problem,' said Rodney

'Here you are'

So as not to alert Rodney's attention to an issue, the Mayor picked up the four pages from the printer and walked over to the water dispenser and helped himself to a glass of water.

'That's been great Rodney' said the Mayor, 'I've always wondered how you guys get all that information from a little box on the wall at my house and change it into a bill in my mailbox. Now I know.'

They shook hands at the main door

'I'm sure Mr. Conroy will be sorry he missed you and will be in touch' said Rodney as the Mayor and the Moron walked out the door

'I'm sure he will' beamed the Mayor

'The crafty bastard' said the Mayor, 'he's been using your ploy ten years ahead of you', but the mechanics are still there. You can use them and still charge the City for the replacement of the meters'

'You are a genius' the Moron said, 'You deserve a hug and perhaps a bit more'

Tuesday morning Tom made the coffee, the Mayor and the boys were round the oval table before the staff came in. The boys were amazed when the Mayor recited the happenings of the day before.

'Now you know why I had to get to you this morning, I am sure my first visitor tomorrow morning will be Mr. Conroy. I need to be prepared.'

After throwing mud at the wall, a piece stuck; George. The person who would get the most benefit in seeing Conroy squirm would be non-other than George.

A quick phone call, George was well onside, he would be at the Mayor's office first thing in the morning. But just in case, how could they link Conroy with receiving money from the water meter company.

Try as they might they couldn't come up with any ideas and really if they did there wasn't time. To act on them.

'Bluff' said Bert. 'It's the only way, bluff the bastard. Let's face it if he sees George there his heart is going to sink. But we need a little more'

Then the Mayor came up with his ace in the hole and showed them his four graphs. He had taken a look at them at home.

'Look at them, they are exactly the same pattern, year over year with one adjustment, there is a standard increase every month of exactly three percent.'

'So, added Bert, let me get this right, 'the meters are all duds, he has a computer program based on the homeowners' readings from the year before he started his fraud. Every month was exactly the same as the previous year and was increased by three percent the following year.'

'He made his money up front from the backhander he received from the water meter manufacturer said Kev. 'then he was clever, not too greedy, I bet he takes a piece of the three percent.'

'Do you think you can handle this, in the morning?' asked Tom

'You bet, said the Mayor, this is going to be a means to an end,' feeling more and more like one of the boys.

Next morning the Mayor and George met really early and after three cups of coffee felt comfortable and confident.

The Mayor sat at his desk twiddling with his pencil, unable to concentrate. I only hope he turns up now after all this he thought.

By the time he got to his office, found out about our visit, vented his spleen, jumped in his car and made it to City Hall, it should be any time now, thought the Mayor

'If he's coming it will be really soon, are you ready' the mayor shouted to George who was sat on the toilet in the mayor's private little wash room.

The door burst open.

'You are a nasty piece of work, conning your way in to the building, intimidating my staff and you hadn't got the balls to tell me' said Conroy as he sat down his face starting to flush like a tomato.

'I hear that you checked over your water use; did you find anything useful', Conroy asked in a patronizing way, not being sure whether the Mayor had or was capable of discovering anything.

'I found enough' said the mayor calmly

'What's that supposed to mean'

'I found enough to figure out that you've been shafting the city for quite a few years'

'And you haven't. said Conroy. 'I warned you that I have enough on you to nail you to the wall' he snarled.

This is where he hoped that Bert's advice, 'Bluff' would work.

'You sneak into my department, con that idiot that works there into showing you stuff on the computer's. By the way because of you he was fired'

The Mayor, calmness personified smiled, 'that's a shame, nice boy, did he know much of what was going on. By the way, I have another friend of yours.'

The Mayor raising his voice called out, 'George, have you a minute.'

George kind of stumbled out of the little wash room

'Who the hell are you?'

'I'm the guy you shafted some nine or ten years ago' said a relaxed George, 'In case you can't remember, I have records of the dummy water meters you wanted manufacturing and how you used my prototype to go to the company in China,' he bluffed.

All of a sudden Conroy came back telling George that his product was a piece of garbage, that's why he went to China to get a better deal for the City.

'So, you do admit that you did get all the meters from China,' said the Mayor

'Certainly, what would you have done'

'I wouldn't have ordered and installed dummy meters'

'You can't prove that'

'You know we can and we can prove that China paid for your Mexican hacienda' again bluffed George

'Bull shit' shouted Conroy,

'Is it' added the Mayor as George put his phone on the table by his side.

'I'll tell you what' said the mayor, 'Why don't you write your letter of resignation right now, George and I will drive you to your office so that you can pick up your personal items and then we will pop you back here so that you can drive home'

The mayor had learnt a lot from the boys, now relaxed he passed a sheet of paper and pen to Conroy, 'a laid-back life in Mexico is better than a stressful life in jail'.

The Mayor was expecting a confrontation and barrage, of insults, but Conroy started writing on the paper the Mayor had placed before him.

George didn't say too much as they drove to meet the boys to explain what had happened

'It couldn't have gone better,' said the Mayor

'Revenge is sweet eh George,' said Bert

'Not really, I wanted to see the bastard in jail'

The boys went on to explain to George the theory about the tape measure of life and that he had quite a bit left, but they, including the Mayor, have much less.

'You can spend the next few years stressed out, going to court, dealing with the press. We would rather see him sail off in to the sunset. Let's face it you think that he is going to spend the rest of his life lying in the sunshine having a great time. Sure, he is going to be comfortable, but his punishment is that being turfed from his comfort zone is going to niggle at his ego for the rest of his days'

George smiled, he realized that if he had of had the chance, he would have gone about it in a whole different way, probably not the right way.

'You know what George' said the Tom, 'you have to realize that we have become quite blasé over the years, as we have helped and mentored many people who have done quite well. However, many of them get to the stage that when they feel you can't help them any further you are superfluous. We could recite the names of the people we know who would not employ us because of our ages, in a way are jealous of our talents and the fact that we know more than they do. If they knew what we were up to, what we have achieved and what we can do they really would be royally pissed off.

'One more question before I am off,' said George

'What's next, do you still want the "knock-offs'

'Well Mr. Mayor' asked the boys.

'Definitely'

George shook their hands, thanked them and headed for the door

The boys told the Mayor that he was right, he had to go for it and laid out the reasons. You owe George, it's a way to pay him back. The wonderful thing is that the infrastructure is already in place, to complete the ploy and of course make the money, you just have command and install the dummy meters. Most importantly though, by helping the Moron with her plan, you will have her by the whatsits.

Jim went on, 'by the way, you had better get over to the utilities department and tell the staff that Mr. Conroy has taken early retirement which you have reluctantly agreed to. Then you should get hold of the young guy that Conroy fired, reappoint him not into his previous position but as the new manager of utilities.'

The Mayor gulped, 'Why?'

'Think about it, you don't want a new person who could discover what is going on. This young kid either knows and doesn't want to say anything or probably hasn't got a clue. You can mentor and nurture him. Then you need to get the Moron to go in or get one of her friends to go in and switch the money process and bank accounts. You should do this straight away as you want to find out how exactly how he did it and make sure no more money is going his way'

'Oh, and one more thing, carried on Jim like a conveyor belt, actually two; announce it at City Hall and of course start working with your girl friend to get her set up.

The Mayor couldn't wait to get to the Moron and amongst other things update her

The cell phone went

'Your table's occupied, I'll keep the oval table for you'

The boys were at the oval table ear plugs in when the Moron walked into Chat and straight to join Gloria at the table.

Fortunately, Bethany was late, so quickly the Moron went over her plan to give Bethany the position of representing the City in the management of its water utilities.

'Do you honestly think that Bethany can handle that'

'Definitely not,' said the Moron.

Gloria chuckled as she realized what the Moron was up to and as Bethany made her way to the table the Moron told Gloria that all will be made clear

The Moron couldn't wait to tell her friends that she was going to put the City on the map as the leader in water sustainability and then care of the environment

'How are you going to manage that' asked Bethany.

'I'm not, you are' said the Moron as she sipped on her prosecco.

The Moron explained that the three of them were going to be a committee to run, the City utilities. 'I have the backing of the Mayor and he suggested that you Bethany because of your insight into environmental issues should lead it.' The self-image and flattery took over, she was bouncing in her chair as the Moron enlightened her on how she would be working with and overseeing the new manager, Rodney.

The Moron was on a mission though.

However, we can go further than that, why don't we incorporate a company and implement a replacement water meter rehabilitation program of our own

The Moron laid it on the table to the ladies. 'We just have to go out and buy thirty thousand water meters.'

'Great, where do we get those from' Gloria asked

'Hold on' said Bethany 'before we check out the meters, don't we need to have the money to buy them',

'Err yeah' uttered the Moron.

'Why don't we try to sweet talk the City in to putting the money up?' suggested Gloria. 'There are three of us, plus your friend the mayor.'

They were sucking up to each other with none of them having a clue what to do next, hoping the other would come up with the answer.

The boys sat at the oval table taking it all in
'Ok, let's get this organized'.

They worked on a plan to benefit themselves and started throwing mud at the wall as the basis of a plan so that they could pass it on to the Mayor who in turn would set up the Moron

'We should ask George how easy the meters are to install' said Kev, and where does the data end up and how is it billed'

'No problem with radio waves as there won't be any. We can suggest that an independent company goes out and checks them out with specialist equipment

With Bethany and Rodney in charge what can go wrong.

A numbered company was incorporated with the ladies as executives of the company. They set up a bank account and were ready to go. The euphoria of having their own company clouded the fact that what they were doing was illegal but they didn't recognize that as they had the opportunity to make a great deal more money than their ex-friend the education paper pusher.

The Moron, with the help of her councillor friends and especially the Mayor, put together the proposal for the city-wide Water Meter Rehabilitation Program. The environmentalists loved it and so did the fiscal members who saw it as another cash grab in that they had another means to grab a bit of extra revenue if the budget was starting to turn a bit sour,

It walked through council with only one vote against it. Even the multi-million-dollar cost was accepted.

The first installment from the City into their numbered company bank account arrived.

The ladies sat in an expensive restaurant, miles away from Mere Folly to toast success. The money and the prosecco were going to their heads and any ramifications and consequences were not even considered.

'I have a meeting with the Mayor and a representative from the water meter manufacturer tomorrow' the Moron said.

Gloria was really into it, 'Sounds good' she said drooling, 'anything you want us to do'

George was introduced to the Moron by the Mayor and showed her the prototypes. 'They are wonderful', she said. George was truly diplomatic, he gave her the invoice, she gave him the cheque. He had noted on the invoice 'imitation boxes for retail use only'. She didn't even read that bit as she was much too pleased to get her hands on the actual article to show it to her committee.

George was straight round to his bank to deposit and at the same time explain why such a big cheque. He told them he had just landed a big contract and to "starch" it straight away, so that he could start production.

When she saw the Moron arrive, Bridget immediately texted the boys as she headed to her table.

A really great move by the Moron thought the boys as they took their seats at the oval table. The boys listened intently as the Moron and the ladies discussed what they were going to do. However, they were really amused by the fact that they had already laid out a chunk of the City's money, almost had 30,000 dummy water meters and hadn't a clue what they were going to do next.

'Soon we are going to have the warehouse full of plastic water meters' said the Moron. We are going to need a team to go from house to house to install them. Let's give it some thought over the next week as to who we hire to do the job. Do you know anybody. Bethany looked at her, 'of course not' she said

The boys were in hysterics at the back of the café. I bet she calls the Mayor now looking for some help or sex or both

Sure enough the Mayor was beckoned.

She told the Mayor that she had done the hard stuff now she had to figure out how to install them, do the monitoring and the billing. He was relaxed as he told her that he would work on it and look after her

He really did mean look after her

In the meantime, the boys sat around the oval table throwing mud at the wall, working on ideas as to how the new committee should re vamp the department under the new management, how it should work and how they could help the ladies to get their water meter program moving.

With all the acquisitions, construction, transformations going on in the background the boys had moved out of their houses. A friend had a condo building under construction and near completion so they ended up renting a unit each until they were able to move in to their new homes.

They met with the Mayor at the condo at the request of the Mayor to discuss whether they were prepared to help with the meter caper.

These women are going to go for this whatever I say,' said the Mayor

'Well let them,' said Bert.

But they all agreed that they couldn't go any further, they have no contacts. Are they going to go on the net to try and find a company that's going to install thirty thousand boxes on the sides of houses? Don't you think the installers are going to twig and say something. They agreed that something had to be done as there was a contract out there and money had changed hands.

'That's their fault for being dumber than two sets of hammers said Kev.

But the Mayor stepped in and said he felt guilty for not helping them when they needed it

Hold on said Tom, you're the one who set the Moron up in the first place and now you want to let her off the hook. Why did you do it in the first place, wasn't it job security. If you don't appear to help her she is going to go after your balls and she will be the Mayor in a few months' time They told the Mayor that he had to go through with it and help the Moron and her friends.

At the suggestion of the boys the mayor met the Moron at the table in Chat. The Mayor was a little guarded as he knew he was being monitored.

'Have you found a company that you can trust to do the installation' asked the mayor.

She admitted in quite a contrite way that she hadn't got a clue.

In his inner most thoughts he was starting to feel sorry for her, but he wasn't going to say anything in front of the boys, just appear hard hearted.

'I'll wrack my brains and see if I can come up with something' He then made the excuse that he had a meeting to go to, she also said she had some things to attend to so after one drink apiece they left.

The boys chatted amongst themselves trying to figure out where they could dig up a way to get the installation done. It was either that or leave the Moron to sink and the Mayor to drown

For once, the Mayor went his way and the Moron hers. The boys were really surprised when the Mayor appeared at the oval table. He waited for the Moron to drive off, saw that the back door was open, drove round the parking lot, parked again and snook in.

'We thought that you two were off to do some loving, said Jim, but we are glad that you are back'

Does anybody know anybody?

The boys and the Mayor didn't want to use anybody locally as the chance of gossip was great. Even using a company within the region created the likelihood of the subterfuge being discovered especially with thirty thousand little projects on the go.

Jim came back from the washroom. 'Something struck me'.

'Did you wee down your leg?' asked Tom.

Jim, as ever, ignored the remark, 'looking at the equipment in there, when taps or the hand dryers or even the piss pots get damaged or outdated, they just take the old ones off and replace them. So, my question is, how easy are they to change, or do they actually have to be changed.

'We have 30,000 houses and 30,000 boxes and the city is splashing out a lot of money, they have to do something,' said Bert.

'But' said Jim, 'Changing them creates more work and the chance that somebody, a householder for instance will watch and see that there is nothing behind the box. Why replace a hollow shell on the wall? Leave the existing box on the wall which everybody believes still works, design the new box so that it fits over the existing box with a special screw and seal. There could be a little box sticking out that gives the impression it contains electronics. A two-minute job'

'Great but won't people ask about the connection to the exiting wiring,' said Kev.

Jim Carried on, he was on a roll, 'it will be explained that, as the new box is wireless the two will work together'

'We know that there's nothing in it,' went on a confused Kev.

'Brilliant, of course not, we know that but everybody else believes the existing boxes do a job, these new boxes are state of the art wireless modules which will monitor water usage much more accurately and help regulate over consumption.'

Tom couldn't believe it, 'Jim I will probably pay for this but just as an apple falling on Newton's head helped him with gravity. As a result of you splashing your boots you have solved the problem of the box installation. You are a genius."

The Mayor was ecstatic. 'We they have thirty thousand of them paid for said the mayor. The homeowners and the city are going to believe they are getting something for their money.'

Tomorrow, Mr. Mayor, advised Bert, you can tell your girlfriend that she will have 30,000 new wireless modules that will be attached over the existing utility box. She and her committee can market the change to the city homeowners.

In the meantime, we will contact George and tell him to re design the boxes to sealed units, still with the security tag on them, a metal identity tag, a simple means to attach them over the existing box and something inside the little box to add a bit of weight.

George knew a company that would hire students on contract to go around Mere Folly installing the boxes.

It's a done deal' said George. 'One thing that concerns me though, you are doing this for nothing, I would like to cut you in, I am doing rather well out of this deal'

'Thanks for the offer' said Bert, 'we are getting other benefits' as he smiled at George who smiled back and nodded.

The boys and the mayor sat at the oval table the next day, very happy in the knowledge that the project was going according to plan and that there was no link between them, the Mayor and the Moron. It was the Moron's project to screw up.

An article explaining the project was be placed in the Boys' newspaper whilst the Mayor explained the concept of the boxes, how they would be installed and by who to the Moron.

'How did you come up with that idea'

'Just lying in bed thinking of you and it just came to me'

He didn't know whether she believed him or not, but for once he really didn't care.

The Moron met with her friends at their table at Chat. The boys were tuned in.

She explained the concept to her committee. 'That's great, how did you think of that idea?' said Bethany. 'I haven't been sleeping very well, lately, and you know how sometimes these things just come to you in the middle of the night, I always have a pad of paper next to my bed, so I wrote it down. As soon as I had done that I went straight to sleep as if a great weight had been lifted off my shoulders.

The boys again were in stitches.

'We know why she hasn't been sleeping much,' said Jim, 'but I suppose she's bought in to the concept.'

'What else could she do, said Tom, 'if it had been left to her, she would still be lying in bed searching for an answer'

'With the odd interruption from the Mayor every now and again,' grinned Bert.

She explained to the ladies that the boxes were now being manufactured to the new specifications.

'We still have the problem of who installs them and have to make sure that it will be done properly. We don't want anybody finding out about the uniqueness of the boxes'

The boys listened intently as the Moron was actually doing a good job of explaining everything.'
'Really though, it doesn't matter who we use to do the installation'

'How come?' asked Bethany

The boys gasped, 'Good job she's not paid to think,' said Jim.

'Think about it' said the Moron, 'all we are looking for is somebody to attach a sealed box over an existing one. They aren't replacing the existing box, that stays, there is no complicated installation, we could even give them a pretend "beeper" so that after installation a button is pressed a green light goes on, it beeps and the installer and the homeowner, if they are watching thinks it's working'

Gloria and Bethany toasted the Moron with prosecco.

'You are a genius' said Gloria as Bethany smiled

The Boys had another sip of their beer happy in the knowledge that another City project was being handled by people who hadn't a clue what they were doing.

22.

When the journey began who'd have thought that the boys would have been involved with a vineyard, a condominium, a newspaper, re-developing a river valley, a downtown refurbishment, control of the mayor, his competitor, even the council, the water utility.

The boys were discussing where to go next. Let's not waste what we have started, let's make sure that all the projects we have in hand are completed. They will then be so much easier to control and we can then look at other projects, but not until.

They still kept their heads on, having worked their way up the ladder the hard way. They had seen so many who had retired, done nothing to do stagnated and then decayed. It was the years in business, the experience in different fields, management of people, having staff who wanted to work with them, the mentoring, the learning, getting away from upper management elitism, that gave them the drive and desire to carry on their journey. The boys got to the stages in their careers where people were jealous of their success, were not true friends and sucked up to them only because they had the authority of decision makers. As soon as the boys left their various positions they became of no use to these so-called friends and any relationship disappeared.

They talked about and learnt from Tom's experience with one particular executive who he really helped, but all the time he was using him as he did most people. From that bad experience life taught him that you can't control someone's loyalty. No matter how good you are to them when you out-serve your use to them it doesn't mean that they will treat you the same. No matter how much they mean to you doesn't mean that they will value you the same

Mere Folly was looking like a construction site, but out of all the projects the condo was leading the way. The boys had decided that for peace on the war front they had to be back living in their own new homes as soon as possible.

The building was a thing of beauty, mainly glass but with a touch of off-white rendering. It was designed and constructed specially to support the rooftop garden with trees on the roof and on the balconies, in fact a miniature urban woodland, with the right plants in the right places helping to clean pollution. The trees attracted birds which of course built were attracted to build their nests there. The roof was specifically constructed with a triple membrane to ensure that there was no mold. The architect used special light soil to help with the weight load and to ensure the soil was oxygenated. Irrigation came from re-circulated waste water in the condo. The garden offered shade, helping to keep the building cool

There were no units on the ground floor, instead the ground floor was an atrium full of trees, plants and flowers given to the local botanical society in return for the provision of care, expertise and design. The fragrance from the flowers and especially the orchids provided a sensual welcome

The four glass walled penthouses, six floors up looked south over to the river valley with the other side of the penthouses facing north and north west with climatic shutters to shut out the odd wind and snow storm from the north. There was a balcony peeping over the vineyard and its courtyard, the café, the shops and restaurant, the building looked like a giant greenhouse rising from its garden. It was paradise sitting on the cafe terrace with a digestif watching the sun set, the light fade and the view disappear.

They were so pleased to finally get into their new homes. The big concern was what the neighbors would think.

The newspaper described the building as exquisite, leading Mere Folly into the leadership position of green urban habitats. A number of neighbors had bought units and others admired it as the building and its surroundings made it the neighborhood in the city.

The remaining few were just plain envious.

People, visitors, tourists, were taking advantage of the areas in which to walk, get exercise, with path ways connecting the vineyard area, the river valley and the downtown.

With no water yet in the river / canal it could be clearly seen ambling through downtown. The weeds, debris, garbage had gone and repairs to the river bank and the pathways gave it a pristine look. Courtyards were laid out, on the riverbank and pathways shops, cafes and restaurants. Mario had done a great job in planning and attracting diverse food businesses to area, foodies were licking their lips in anticipation.

The newspaper was buoyant with feature articles describing the virtues of the city, how it will look, all driving advertising revenue as businesses sought to take advantage and move in

Downtown, the cutesy stores, the art galleries, the artisan workshops were coming back, more restaurants were opening, the foodies were forking out to eat in Mere Folly. The parking lots and shuttle buses were doing their jobs, citizens, tourists and sightseers were wandering the sites imagining the finished article.

Flat bottom colourful boats had been specially deigned and were now being delivered. The boats would slowly saunter backwards and forwards up and down the canal giving passengers a view and feel of the downtown from the inside. Not only were the passengers being presented with a whole different perspective, but they were also being transported from west of city hall eastward about a mile. From there it was a short walk out of the river valley past artisan workshops and a garden centre, to the vineyard, with its shops, restaurants and cafes.

The citizens were liking what they were seeing not only with the infrastructure of the city but the fact that the slugs who were causing the city to stagnate were being weeded out. They hadn't a clue what was happening behind the scenes but perception was everything.

The pastel shaded crossings, a local joke, that were not visible especially when covered with snow and snud were allowed to wear out. Flashing warning lights and floodlights shining directly on to the crossings were installed. They became known as "Mayor's Crossings" the general public were thrilled.

The Mayor, as the only candidate, was re-elected, he had promised reduced residential property taxes and against the grain for an elected official he actually kept his word as they decreased significantly.

The boys still met every Friday afternoon, buying tickets and dreaming about winning the lottery, but there was absolutely no way that they could have envisioned winning the big prize in the way they had done. It gave them inspiration to now continue and see the projects completed. They knew where they were going for the time being, they didn't know what the future held or for that matter how long the tape was.

God only knows what's in store…….

Manufactured by Amazon.ca
Acheson, AB